## About the Author

I was born in Calcutta (now called Kolkata), India. I have always loved writing stories and reading books of any type but mainly crime fiction/CSI. I am married, my second time around and have three children from my first marriage. I now have three grandsons and a little granddaughter born in May 2019.

My husband, Peter, is my rock and inspiration, as are my three children who have always given me their support in whatever I do and who spurred me on to write my book.

# Catch A Killer - If You Can!

**Millie Dent**

# Catch A Killer - If You Can!

Olympia Publishers
*London*

www.olympiapublishers.com
OLYMPIA PAPERBACK EDITION

Copyright © Millie Dent 2020

The right of Millie Dent to be identified as author of
this work has been asserted in accordance with sections 77 and 78
of the Copyright, Designs and Patents Act 1988.

**All Rights Reserved**

No reproduction, copy or transmission of this publication
may be made without written permission.
No paragraph of this publication may be reproduced,
copied or transmitted save with the written permission of the
publisher, or in accordance with the provisions
of the Copyright Act 1956 (as amended).

Any person who commits any unauthorised act in relation to
this publication may be liable to criminal
prosecution and civil claims for damage.

A CIP catalogue record for this title is
available from the British Library.

ISBN: 978-1-78830-454-2

This is a work of fiction.
Names, characters, places and incidents originate from the writer's
imagination. Any resemblance to actual persons, living or dead, is
purely coincidental.

First Published in 2020

**Olympia Publishers
Tallis House
2 Tallis Street
London
EC4Y 0AB**

Printed in Great Britain

# Dedication

Special dedication to my ever-patient husband, Peter, my children and my parents, to whom I owe everything, especially my mother, who encouraged me so much to not give up and who sadly passed away before she could see me realise my dream.

# Introduction

I suppose we've all heard someone say at some time in their life *"It was destiny* or *I had no choice, it was fate"* — trust me when I say that this is not true. We make our own destiny and we choose to do the things that we do. Remember, for every action there is a consequence.

Every killer has a history that they would like to blame on various reasons for why they are the way they are and why they did the things they did; blaming their personality; bad upbringing; being bullied at school, etc. etc. etc., I hope you enjoy my fictional read as it takes you into the mind of a brutal, psychopathic killer, who believes he is beyond the reach of justice.

# Chapter One

I had a perfectly happy childhood within a moderate, middle-class family, with a father who worked his butt off to keep us fed and watered, so to speak, and a mother who doted on me and my sister. Mum never worked so she had plenty of time to give her attention to her family, which we loved, so no, I can't blame anything on a bad childhood; it was maybe my puberty years when I needed the guidance that I lacked. I was certainly never bullied at school or later in the workplace either.

No, my story starts in the summer of 1977, when I discovered the meaning of 'love' — or so I thought.

It was a late July evening; I was about fifteen at the time and my hormones were starting to kick off, making me restless and not knowing what was happening to my body. My mum couldn't explain to me what I was going through and my father (being old school) told me to talk to my mother about the 'birds and bees' — all I wanted was someone to explain what was happening to me. A boy of fifteen going through puberty needs an adult to advise him of how he should treat a person of the opposite sex — actually, using the word sex seemed odd to me but, hell, if nobody was going to tell me, I suppose I would have to find out for myself.

When I saw the face of my angel (or so I thought) she was sitting waiting for the bus just fiddling with her hair as she had done in class for the last two years. She never appeared to notice me at all, but then, I was always fairly quiet, not knowing what to say. I found out later that her name was Becky and she actually lived about two streets away from me, in Hackney.

I walked up to her and asked her if she was waiting for the bus — how lame is that! What else would she be waiting for! — jeez, what a chat line!

Becky turned and smiled at me and suddenly, I felt this overwhelming desire to take her in my arms and kiss her — what was happening, I was only fifteen, should I be feeling this way? What would I do if she let me kiss her? I never got the opportunity to take this conversation any further as Tom Redburn came up and sat down beside her. Tom was the class bully and macho Mr Wonderful but he never bullied me, in fact, he seemed to be a bit wary of me. Don't know why, mind you, I was nothing special.

Tom asked Becky if she was going to the gala ball at the end of school term and if so, did she want to go with him. Becky seemed embarrassed by this request and told Tom she would think about it and get back to him. As the bus approached, Tom stepped in front of Becky, stopping her from getting on the bus. She looked at me for help, so I walked over and told Tom to stop acting like a moron and let her board the bus.

"What's it to you?" said Tom.

I stepped up to him and pulled myself up to my full six feet and said, "I guess you must be short of hearing, I said let her be."

Tom decided I was not a push-over and moved out of the way. "I just wanted to help her on board — what's your problem?" said Tom.

"Nothing — stop being an ass all your life, Tom," I said.

Becky got on board and took her seat, with Tom moving in right beside her, making sure there was no space for a third person to sit. Becky looked over her shoulder and mouthed the words, "Thank you," to me, which made me feel like some kind of hero.

I never saw much of Becky that day and made a promise to myself to keep a watch out for her. When I got home from school that day my mum said that Becky had called round (I didn't even know she knew where I lived — wow!) She had left a note for me to meet her at Franks Park — our local park where youngsters hung out with kids their own age. She said she would meet me at seven p.m. so I told my mum I was just going around to a friend's house to do some studying for our end-of-term exams.

I was so excited; it was all I could do to eat my dinner that evening before seeing her. I pinched some of my dad's aftershave and dabbed it all over me, after I had a shower. I told my mum I was showering early as I would probably be late and didn't want to disturb anyone when I got in, she seemed to accept it.

## Chapter Two

I waited until eight thirty p.m. and realised that she was never turning up. I was now quite angry and felt such a fool — what on earth was this all about? What did she take me for?

As I strolled back towards the exit gates to the park, I heard a cry or should I say, a whimper, like someone crying softly. I stopped and listened again in case I had been mistaken but no, there it was again. I walked over to the bushes near the exit and saw a pair of legs sticking out from under the bushes. On approaching the body, I saw Becky lying on the ground. Her clothes were torn, and her skirt had been pulled halfway up her body. I was so shocked I didn't know what to say first.

"Oh my God, Becky, what happened? Who did this to you? Tell me — I'll fucking kill them!" I shouted.

"I didn't see him, I only know he came from behind me as I was coming to meet you and he pulled me down to the ground and started to tear my blouse, he was so strong and kept me facing the other way the whole time he was on top of me. He said he would make sure nobody would ever want me again because I was such a whore and a tease! I started to scream but he knocked me out and I just woke up and found you here," she sobbed.

I picked Becky up and decided to take her home to my parents to see what they could do. She didn't want me to call the police because she knew she would be in trouble as she was supposed to be at a friend's house studying (same as me) and her parents would be furious with her.

My mum was clearly shocked when she saw us both at the front door. Mum and Dad both said the police needed to be advised and Becky needed to be in hospital getting examined by a Police Medical Examiner. Becky started to scream and say she couldn't do this and please don't say anything to anyone — please.

Becky phoned her mum and said she would be staying overnight at her friend's house and would this be okay, it obviously was, so Mum made up the bed in the spare room and she would stay there for the night. I helped Becky up to the room and Mum gave her something of my sister's to wear to bed. She said she would shower, and Mum left her upstairs with me to talk to her. Becky got undressed in my sister's room and came out of the bedroom to go to the bathroom in nothing but a towel. I couldn't help noticing the electricity that passed between us with just a meeting of eyes. She looked so beautiful, even after what she had just suffered. I couldn't take my eyes off her and I suddenly felt this hardening in my groin, which I hoped she hadn't noticed, but which definitely would keep me awake that night, just dreaming about her.

# Chapter Three

After Becky had showered and gone to her bedroom, I asked her if she wanted something to drink before she slept, and she agreed a hot chocolate would be nice. I made this and brought it up to her. When I entered the bedroom, she was already in bed with the duvet pulled up to her shoulders. She said that she felt a lot calmer now and wanted to thank my parents for letting her stay overnight. She turned to pick up the mug of hot chocolate and touched my hand very gently, which sparked something inside of me, which I was finding very hard to control.

I spluttered something like, "Oh, sorry," but she never moved her hand away, instead, she held onto it and pulled me closer to her.

"Perhaps I should say thank you properly for helping me tonight, you were quite my hero, so thank you," she said, as she pulled me near and planted the most delicious and passionate French kiss on my lips — OMG, she knew how to French kiss — what else did she know, I was wondering. My mind was racing ahead of itself — hang on a minute, I thought — she's been through a hell of an ordeal, perhaps this was just shock or something. Hell, how would I know, all I did know was that I was having one almighty hard-on!

Becky drew away from me for breath and asked me if I had ever kissed a girl before and, being the idiot liar that I am, I said yes.

"Well, you know where this can lead, don't you?" she said provocatively, letting the duvet fall from her shoulders and revealing her perfectly naked body beneath. The warning bells were ringing in my ears because she should not be doing this.

"What are you doing, Becky — you must be in shock, surely," I said.

"I just want to know if you still find me attractive — he said nobody would want me once he had finished with me," she cried. "I know you want me. I've seen you watching me at school, that's why I arranged to meet with you, and I wanted to see how far we could take this and if you were really interested in me," she said.

So that is what this was all about — she just wanted to know if I found her attractive still — all this teasing was for her ego. Were all girls like this? Is that what they do? Prick tease a guy until he's dizzy with testosterone and then expect him not to want to screw them?

I got up and walked out of the room. I told my mum I was going to bed. As I lay in my bed, I decided that I was never going to be used like this again — jeez, I was only fifteen, what did they expect!

The next day, Becky went back to her home and went to school as if nothing had happened. Certainly nothing would ever happen between us — I made sure of that. Tom Redburn seemed to suddenly be Becky's 'best friend' and I often wonder now if it was him who attacked Becky and left her there — anyway, she seemed to love the attention he was giving her. I never did go to the gala ball at the end of term, and quite frankly, I didn't really miss it. If I'm honest, I did miss seeing Becky around but she was a red rag to a bull and my hormones couldn't take a distraction like that anymore — I was too young for such strong feelings — after all, there was a whole world out there to explore and I was sure I would find my perfect partner when the time was right.

## Chapter Four

Three years passed since that night with Becky, we never spoke about what happened and our paths at school never really crossed again, how foolish of me to think she would be the love of my teenage years — dah!

It is now 1980, and I am working for my father in his garage as a technician. I'm doing an apprenticeship in order to make my mum and dad proud and also to get me out of here. I am eighteen years old and have had several girlfriends but seem to have a keen desire to step up my career status. I should qualify as a technician by the end of 1982 and will look to work for the big-time car manufacturers out there. I found out in my earlier years that I have a gift for drawing cars not just any old cars but new designs with new features etc., anyway, my dad said he would help further my career any way he can so I look forward to that.

It was in April 1982 that my career and ambitions took a nosedive. I came home early from the garage to get some lunch. (My dad had left me in charge for the day as he needed some time off with Mum, he said.) When I opened the back door, I found it strange that there was no sound of Mum or Dad around or my sister, who usually came home for lunch from school. I went upstairs and heard them in the bedroom — OMG, my parents were at it in broad daylight. What were they like! I opened their bedroom door to tell them to keep the noise down and found my dad in bed with another woman — who looked very much like our next-door neighbour, Jan, whose daughter I had slept with on several occasions.

"What the hell are you doing here? Why aren't you at the garage?" my dad shouted.

"And why aren't you with mum?" I shouted.

"Your mum has gone out — you weren't supposed to see this — I'm so sorry, son — please don't tell your mum — it would break her," he begged.

"Get that piece of trash out of our house and out of your bed, you bastard!" I shouted back.

Jan got her clothes on pretty damn quick and almost ran out of the bedroom.

"You are such a liar, how long has this been going on with that woman and WHY?" I shouted.

My dad tried to explain that it was just sex nothing else and that Mum wasn't always interested. I sat at the end of their bed trying to get my head around all that I had seen. What a mess! What was I going to do? I couldn't look at my father again and I could never trust anything he ever said again.

I got up and stormed back to the garage. I gave the other techs the afternoon off and closed the garage up. I went home and told my dad I was leaving and needed money out of my savings account now — I was twenty years of age and needed to get away and think things through. My dad was at his wits end, he wasn't sure what I was going to do with regards to telling my mum what had happened and had been happening for quite a while, it would appear.

Dad gave me my savings book and said that I was able to withdraw monies now that I was over eighteen. He looked genuinely saddened by my leaving but that didn't bother me, I was disgusted to think that he had been deceiving Mum all these years whilst I always thought they were perfectly happy. As I said earlier, I did have a perfectly happy childhood, but the child was now a man, and it was time to move on.

## Chapter Five

It is now some time since I left home. Remembering that day only saddens me as I left behind my little sister and Mum with a letter saying I was going out into the world to seek my fortune. Yeah, right!

I put myself through evening school to learn about law and justice and being a policeman. I found that I was a very good student when it came to learning about how to uphold the law and decided that I would like to be a policeman so I studied for the relevant exams. I did eventually pass out at Hendon Police Academy and wrote and told my parents, although I never got a response from them — didn't really expect one.

I worked the beat as a local copper in Streatham Vale where I lived but found that I really wanted to be a Detective in the Special Crimes unit, so I took any courses I could to make the grade. It took a few years, but I eventually got my DC status and here I was, now thirty-two years of age and loving every minute of it.

My parents have never contacted me, but my sister writes to me and says how much she has always missed me and would like us to get together for lunch maybe. I think I'll pass on that — I'm not one for family reunions and would rather be on my own at the moment.

Moving on, I have now been given the onerous task of trying to catch a serial killer who appears to have escaped the law for at least a decade. My team of special agents were gathering all the evidence of his latest victim and I would be apprised of all the details.

I decided to speak to my superintendent about this serial killer to see if he had any ideas on how to catch him. The killer didn't leave any trace of DNA; no fingerprints, blood — nothing to work on. Superintendent Max Stoller was very clever at looking into the psyche of serial killers and had helped on many occasions to solve crimes where a serial killer had been involved but this case was proving difficult, even for him.

# Chapter Six

It was a beautiful Monday morning in London and Sarah Davis, as she now called herself, was on her way to an interview for a job as a legal partner with a company called Golding & Golding Solicitors; she had to make this work, she would make sure that she was someone that was unforgettable to them. At least, that is what she always told herself — she made it her vocation in life to make sure that anyone who met her would always remember her!

    Sarah had decided many years ago that her life was going nowhere so she decided to change her name and has never looked back. As she walked through the doors of Golding & Golding Solicitors, she took in the beautiful surroundings of the building and office. Sarah noticed a young man waiting in reception, who she found out from the receptionist, was called Robert and was another candidate for the same position, well whatever the outcome she was certain that they would meet again and she would get to know him better.

    Sarah thought that she could certainly make her mark here. Her years of studying to be a lawyer had finally paid off and she was heading for the big time. No longer would she have to pretend to be servile to men in order to claw her way to the top of her league — she had finally managed to get there on her own volition and here is where she would stay. She didn't care about who she upset on her way to reach the top — it was her time now, so watch out!

As Sarah was summoned into the office of Steven Golding, her first instinct was, *wow — he's good looking and young, as well. Bet he's married with a gorgeous wife and kids. Anyway, this will not deter me.*

During her interview with Steven, she noticed how he kept giving her sideway glances and wondered if he was attracted to her — she wouldn't be surprised as she had found out in her puberty days that most men were attracted to her two main assets — her breasts. Sarah had realised at an early age that using these assets opened all sorts of doors for her in her career climb and it looked like this would just be another final climb for her. *Ah well,* she thought. *A girl has to do what a girl has to do to get anywhere in life, I suppose — bring it on!*

## Chapter Seven

When her interview was over, Sarah got up to leave Steven's office, but he stopped her and said that he would let her know if she had been shortlisted and could he have a contact number for her. Sarah knew what he meant by this but gave him her mobile number any way.

As she left the building, Sarah walked to her favourite bar near Golding & Golding Solicitors. God, she really needed a drink. She asked the barman for a G&T with ice and a slice and sat in a booth. Sarah took stock of her options right now, reliving the interview with Mr Steven Golding. She considered herself a fairly good judge of character, but Steven was an enigma and a challenge, she would wait and see what the rest of the day panned out like.

She got up and walked over to the bathroom and looked at herself in the mirror. Her long blonde hair and blue eyes were a man magnet and she never failed to turn heads wherever she went. Although in the past, it had got her into some difficult situations — of which, she did not like to think about.

She applied more lipstick and freshened up her appearance, pulled her very tight dress down a few inches, decided she looked great and started to walk out of the bathroom and through the lounge of the bar. When she was halfway across, a voice called out to her.

"Hi, Sarah, would you like a drink or two?" It was Steven, he had finished his interviews he said and was having a quick liquid lunch break. She said she would love a G&T and he moved her over to a booth where he sat very close to her. "So, Sarah, how do you think you did at your interview? Do you have any further questions for me or is there anything I can do for you?" Steven said.

Sarah asked Steven if he and the board had made a decision yet even though she knew what the answer would be.

"Well, it's funny you should say that but there are only 3 other board members plus me and my wife, who is a sleeping partner, so to speak and pardon the pun," he laughed.

"Oh, okay — have you made a decision then?" she said.

"Well, yes and no. Firstly, I need to run some reference checks on you and secondly I have also interviewed another candidate but I'm sure I can re-look at both profiles before I make a final decision and besides we haven't finished our drinks yet — drink up," he said.

Sarah and Steven drank quite a few more drinks and Sarah realised that she was perhaps a little bit tipsy. It was now two thirty p.m. but as Sarah stood up to leave, she realised she could no longer drive her car, she was in no fit state, so Steven said he would get a taxi for her and get them to drop her off at her premises.

Sarah didn't argue as she was in no fit state to drive. However, Steven saw an opportunity to now find out where she lived and she didn't want that — not yet, so she gave the taxi man a bogus address. Now was not the time for her to reveal where she lived to anyone.

When she eventually arrived home, she went straight to bed and turned off her mobile phone. When she awoke later that night, she had several messages on her mobile, one of which was from Steven advising her that the position for a legal partner at his law firm could be hers but he needed to speak with the other board members before a final decision is made and it may be that another position could be involved but he asked if she could-ring him back as soon as possible to discuss this further.

After she showered, she got herself dressed in her favourite red silk dress and decided to telephone her sister to see if she wanted to come out and celebrate her new job. Her sister didn't pick up, so she left a message on her voicemail to get back to her.

Then she phoned Steven and when he answered the phone, she got the impression that he seemed rather annoyed with her.

"You gave the taxi man a wrong address this afternoon — what are you playing at?" he shouted down the phone. "I came round to see if you were okay and was advised that you have never lived there, what game are you playing, young lady?"

"I'm so sorry, Mr Golding, I just don't know you that well and didn't want to give out my address just yet — can you forgive me?" she said in her childlike manner, which always worked for her.

"Of course, but don't scare me like that again," he said.

"Sorry, I was just phoning regarding the message you left and the other candidate involved too," she said.

"Great, how about we celebrate this evening. Are you doing anything or are you with someone?"

"No, nobody. What did you have in mind?" she said — as if she didn't know.

Steven said he would meet Sarah at The Ivy along the embankment for dinner at eight p.m. He could pick her up if she wanted, but Sarah decided to play safe and take a taxi herself. She could drink without worrying about driving.

When Sarah arrived at The Ivy, there wasn't a male around that wasn't looking at her and she felt great. Everything seemed to be falling into place now. She walked over to the table where Steven got up and welcomed her with a kiss on either cheek.

*Wow — he's a bit forward*, she thought. *Only known him a few hours and already kissing on the cheek!*

After some small talk, the conversation got around to the new job offer on the table. Steven told her that it would be a 'sleeping partner' position, which isn't what she expected. She had the qualifications to become a partner and had actually got some money to invest in the business as well, but Steven wasn't listening to all of this, he was finding it hard to keep his emotions under control at the moment.

## Chapter Eight

After they had finished their meal, Steven asked Sarah if she would like to go clubbing, he was at a loose end, his wife was out of town… blah blah, she had heard it all before but what the hell, he was her boss now and this was a ladder she wanted to climb!

She agreed and they went to some nightclubs in Piccadilly, where Sarah realised that Steven was well known by reputation.

After dinner, Steven asked Sarah if she would like to come to his flat in Sloane Street that he used when he was in town. He told Sarah that he lived in the country in Hertfordshire and used this flat as a stopover on Friday nights or whenever he needed to. His wife had no idea he had this flat as he purchased it without her knowledge. Sarah found herself intrigued and decided she was always up for adventure.

As Steven opened the door to the flat, Sarah was immediately impressed by the sheer opulence of the furnishings and decorating. This was an expensive 'pad' and she hoped to have something like this herself one day.

Steven asked her if she wanted a drink to which Sarah replied, "That would be great, do you have a margarita?"

"Not a problem — one margarita coming up," said Steven.

After some small talk and several margaritas later, Sarah decided that perhaps it may be best if she went home and would Steven please put her in a taxi as she didn't bring her car. Steven then moved a bit closer to her on the sofa and asked her if she wanted to stay rather than go home, after all, he felt as if they had become quite good friends and they were both at a loose end. He reached for Sarah's arm to draw her closer to him and she moved a bit closer to him, as she didn't dislike the idea of sleeping with Steven, after all, he was quite handsome and very fit! She said yes, she would stay a bit longer and Steven picked her up and carried her to the bedroom. By this time, Sarah was aware that she perhaps had drunk just a bit too much but what the hell, he's the boss; he can call the shots for now until she says it's time to go.

Steven proved to be a very forceful lover but without any passion, a bit of a 'wham bam and thank you, mam' type of guy. Not at all what she expected! After several hours of continuous sex, which is all it really was, Steven rolled over and fell asleep, leaving Sarah not really knowing what to expect next time, if there was a next time!

Sarah got dressed and left Steven sleeping in the apartment. She definitely wanted to make this guy a better lover, improve his technique if she could, otherwise, she couldn't see any future at all. She wasn't prepared to have sex with him on a long-term commitment if he couldn't improve his sexual prowess. She flagged down a taxi and went home, wondering what Monday would bring for her.

# Chapter Nine

Robert decided that it was time for him to make a change in his life. He, too, had applied for the position of legal partner at Golding & Golding and was hoping that his long-time pal from University days would remember him and help him out on this occasion, after all, he knew stuff about Steven that he wouldn't want anyone else to know.

While he waited in the boardroom for Steven to conduct the interview, he thought about those days and how everything seemed too simple and easy back then and hoped that his life was now about to make a turn in the right direction.

Robert came from a middle-class upbringing where you lived from day-to-day without any 'special rewards' for achieving anything in life. His mother worked as a nurse at the local cottage hospital in Belvedere and his father was a technician, who didn't earn loads of money but managed to keep Robert and his three brothers fed and grateful for whatever they got.

When Robert was eighteen, he decided he wanted to become a lawyer so told his parents he would like to go to university in London UCLA. They were so proud of him and his father worked hard to make sure he could give his eldest son this opportunity that he had never been able to achieve.

Robert went to university at UCLA and had to live in halls of residence rather than travel back and forth to Belvedere. This was another expense to his parents, to which he was eternally grateful. He met Steven there who was also studying law and they became great friends. During the years to follow, Robert and Steven were seen as inseparable and attended every party together and there were plenty of parties in those first two years and not much studying!

Robert found that he had a developed a deep affection for Steven but not in terms of being a homosexual, he just felt very protective towards Steven, a bit like a younger brother, which he now realised he never really needed to be — Steven was quite capable of looking after himself, as he would soon find out.

In their third year at university and several mid-term parties later, Robert and Steven were invited to a party where some new young ladies had just enrolled at the university and were not shy in presenting themselves. Robert found himself attracted to one of them, called Samantha, she was very attractive with eyes that gave a guy the 'come on over here' look, whilst Steven was attracted to the leader of the pack, Felicia, who was totally the opposite in looks, blonde, blue-eyed with legs that went all the way up to her armpits as the saying goes.

They arranged to meet the girls at their party and were looking forward to a very good night! However, things didn't go quite according to plan.

The party was in full swing when they arrived, both Robert and Steven noticed that there were lots of young ladies present who were obviously getting very drunk, very early into the party, with guys who were equally already drunk and some who they noticed were taking drugs, an area both Robert and Steven were not familiar with and who both thought was not their 'thing'.

Robert tried to find Samantha and was not disappointed when he did — wow, she looked fabulous, dressed in a very tight-fitting, skimpy red dress that didn't leave a great deal to the imagination. Robert was still a virgin but had never told Steven or anybody this, he was keeping himself for the 'right' girl. He didn't make a habit of sleeping around just because he was at uni and he didn't believe Steven did either — how wrong he was about Steven on that score!

Sam (as she liked to be called) found herself attracted to Robert in a way she had never felt either, but her feelings for Robert were not as strong as his so she knew she had to play it gently, she didn't want to hurt his feelings, just enjoy her time at uni. Anyway, it was a party, so she decided to have a good time. Robert was such a gentleman and very fit, he clearly looked after himself, he was intelligent and had a bright future and was also such fun. Robert gave Sam a big kiss, full on the lips and found himself drowning in his feelings. He wasn't quite sure where this was all going but decided to go with it until he heard otherwise.

After several drinks and dancing very close together, Robert and Sam decided to go looking for Steven and Felicia to see if they wanted to leave the party and find somewhere more private and not so noisy. They didn't have to search for too long. They found Steven with Felicia in the back garden on the grass, with Felicia not looking very happy as to where Steven was going with his hands. He had his hands up her skirt and was getting very angry that Felicia was resisting him, after all, she was the one who had instigated all this, flirting and rubbing her hands over his well-toned body, telling him how great he was and how fit he was. He was yelling at her to stop fighting and just go with it and to stop being a tease. Robert was visibly shocked at Steven's behaviour and ran over to him and pulled him off, saying this was not what he expected from his friend and he should be careful in case Felicia decided to shout rape, because that is what it was leading to. Robert also noticed that Steven was not fully 'all there'; he seemed dazed, his speech was slurry and he wondered if he had taken some drugs at the party.

He told Sam he was going to take him home and apologised to her for letting her down, but this was not the Steven he knew and he wanted to make sure he could get him back to their halls of residence before anything else kicked off here. Sam said she understood and both guys left, leaving Sam and Felicia available for the rest of the evening to whoever wanted them, not that they would say anything to the guys — hell, no.

When Robert got Steven back to their rooms, he passed out on his bed raving on about how the bitch, Felicia, had led him on and he would make her pay for it, nobody did that to him and got away with it, nobody.

The next day was Sunday and Robert got up to make his breakfast and went to wake up Steven to see if he wanted some, only to find that he was not where he had left him that night — he was nowhere to be found. *Oh well, he was a big boy now*, Robert thought, *and he would have to take care of himself.* But Robert had to admit that Steven's behaviour last night was not what he had expected.

However, later that day Robert noticed that police were calling on campus asking if anyone had seen two girls in a photo they were showing around — the girls turned out to be Felicia and Sam. *Oh my god,* thought Robert. *What had happened to them? And where was Steven?* He had not seen anything of him all day.

When they approached Robert, he told them that Sam was his girlfriend and Felicia was Steven's and they were at the party last night with them and had left them both and come home (he didn't give all the details, after all, he didn't want to get his mate into trouble over nothing that really happened). He was questioned for some time in his residence and the police said that they would get the story confirmed by other witnesses and get back to him, but he should stay close to home in case the girls contacted him or Steven. They asked where Steven was, and Robert said that he had gone out for an early morning run and he would let the police know when he returned. They seemed happy with this and then left.

Robert started to panic after they left and got dressed and went looking for Steven. He found him eventually at the park on a bench fast asleep. He woke him up and asked him what he was doing here and why did he leave his room in the early hours of the morning without telling him, he wasn't in a fit state to be walking anywhere. Steven got to his feet and said he didn't remember anything, last night was a blur and could he help him back to his room, which Robert did.

When they got back to his room and Steven took off his jacket, Robert noticed Steven's t-shirt was blood-stained and wondered if he had fallen and hurt himself on his late-night adventures. However, when Steven took off his t-shirt, Robert noticed there were no marks on his body at all and he became concerned for his friend.

Robert decided he would ask Steven more questions after he had rested and when he was more alert and able to answer properly just to make sure that he got his story straight for the police.

About mid-day, Steven awoke and got showered. He came into their lounge and had a black coffee that Robert had made for him. Robert immediately started to question him about his t-shirt and where did the blood come from and whose blood was it anyway?

## Chapter Ten

Steven looked confused and scared at the same time, saying he didn't know whose blood it was or why he was even on the bench where Robert found him. He didn't remember anything from leaving the party last night and waking up on the bench. Robert decided it was down to him to prepare Steven for his talk with the police and to make sure he stuck to his story, otherwise he would become their first suspect in finding the missing girls — their girlfriends!

This news flash about the girls brought Steven back to reality pretty quickly. Suddenly, he became very quiet as if thinking through something and Robert was scared that he was withdrawing into himself and not able to converse and relay the story to the police properly. Robert was not prepared to lose his position at university because Steven couldn't keep it in his trousers for one night (something that still shocked Robert, who hadn't realised his pal was putting it around so much with the ladies). He had worked hard for the last three years and wanted to make sure he got his law degree, so he wasn't about to let this all fall apart now neither was he going to let his friend down either — *what a bloody mess*! he thought.

They rehearsed their stories, which other students had corroborated so it looked like it was plain sailing from here on in. Steven said he would burn the t-shirt in the school incinerator so there was no trace of it to be found anywhere and both agreed this was best thing to do.

Robert and Steven never talked about this again and the police accepted their statements and kept the missing girls on their files. Robert was very sad that he never had the chance to take things further with Sam, but Steven didn't seem too bothered about missing Felicia and soon found another girl to party with. Robert would find out, years later, the truth about his friend, Steven, which would answer the many questions that Steven had refused to answer, until now.

## Chapter Eleven

Robert was brought back to reality when Steven entered the boardroom.

"My goodness," he said. "You look really well, old friend. How's life treating you?" said Steven.

"Not too bad. You've certainly come up in the world, Steven, doing well for yourself," said Robert.

"Yes, and I believe that's why you're here, for this partnership vacancy, am I correct?" said Steven.

"Well, I thought I would see if an old friend would be interested in helping out another old friend," said Robert.

Steven said he was more than happy to help out Robert and said his profile and CV were spot on for the role and he would consider him and get back to him.

Robert said, "Is that it? You will consider me after all I've done for you. I think you owe me more than that, Steven, don't you? Or have you forgotten?"

Steven told Robert that perhaps they could meet for dinner to discuss this further and said he would get his secretary to arrange dinner at The Ivy for seven thirty p.m. tonight, if he was able to make it. Steven told Robert that he had also considered another applicant for this position (he quite liked to play games with people, especially knowing how desperate Robert & Sarah were for the position) and perhaps they could all meet up socially.

Robert agreed and then left. He thought he was going to have a nice long chat with an old friend but clearly that is not what Steven wanted, but he would give him the benefit of the doubt and see what else he was going to discuss this evening.

When both men arrived at The Ivy for dinner, Sarah was already there and she also noticed that Steven looked uncomfortable and ill at ease with Robert (who Sarah had already met when she came for her interview with Steven and unbeknown to Steven, Robert and Sarah had already got to know each other better) and was anxious to find out why.

"Okay," said Steven. "Let's start. First of all, I am going to offer you Robert, the position of junior paralegal in our office not the business partnership and Sarah would be a Junior Partner. I believe you are both suitable for these positions and who knows, perhaps in a year or so I can re-consider your positions and look to promote you both."

Robert was totally dumbfounded, words failed him. He thought he was getting the partnership position, but even this was better than nothing and things could change in a year's time. Sarah could see that Robert was not too happy but she thought that the partnership position would be hers if she played her cards right with Steven, after all a girl has to do what a girl has to do…

"Well, this calls for a celebration, don't you think?" said Steven. "Come on, let's go party!"

All three of them sat down to eat and Steven and Robert talked about their uni days, which made Steven feel very uncomfortable. Sarah was interested to find out why when she had Steven to herself, later. Yes, there were quite a few questions she wanted to ask him.

"What's the matter, Steven?" said Robert. "You don't need to worry about me spilling the beans after all these years, no worries, man, you've done good by me and I appreciate it, will always be there for you when you need me as well."

"Thanks, Rob, I know I can count on you," said Steven. "Now, let's pay the bill and get out of here."

All three left The Ivy and made their way to the Soho district, where there were plenty of clubs they could frequent and plenty of ladies and men on tap, so to speak.

Late Saturday morning, when Robert finally got back to the apartment that Steven had said he could use, he phoned his mother to tell her about his new position and as usual, was comforted in the support she always gave him. She said she would like to know when he would be coming home for a weekend and Robert declined saying he was too busy now. He felt bad when he finally came off the phone, but hell, he was enjoying himself too much and as much as he loved his mum and family, he loved his independence and his new lifestyle.

After a pretty quiet Saturday, Robert decided to call Sarah to see if she was busy and would she care for a coffee Sunday morning. Her phone just went to voicemail, so he left her a message to call him back.

Meanwhile back in her apartment, Sarah was listening to Robert's voicemail message and thinking that it was now her time and Monday would prove to be a more productive day than today. Steven had been very accommodating and was obviously expecting great things from her — it was her time to shine!

## Chapter Twelve

Detective James Bolton was at the forensic research offices to see if there were any further updates on the latest victim of the serial killer — five women had been killed, all brutally murdered and sexually abused after they had been killed, even more horrendous. James often thought of his little sister when incidents like this occurred. Mind you, she wouldn't be that little any more, but he still worried, nonetheless. He called his mum to ask how the family was and she confirmed all was okay and asked how he was, the usual small talk. James loved his family, but still found it hard to forgive his father for deceiving his mother so long ago.

James phoned his sister, Laurie, and asked her if she wanted to come to dinner that night. Laurie was so excited that her brother had called her — since he graduated from the police academy at Hendon, he had not had much time for her, so this was really cool she thought. She was so proud of her brother — getting out of the East End of London was such a step up the ladder and she couldn't think of anyone who deserved it more than her brother, James, who said he would pick her up at seven p.m. from her home.

James was amazed at how grown up his little sister was when she opened the door. She was so beautiful. "You look lovely, sis," he said. "Wow, I'd forgotten how beautiful you were."

"Why thank you, big brother," said Laurie.

"Mum and Dad, James is here," she shouted.

"Is Mikey around?" said James.

"No, he's probably out, up to no good," said his dad, looking like he'd just stepped out of the shower. "How are you, son?" he said to James.

"Oh, I'm fine," said James, seeing his mum in the kitchen he walked past his dad and gave his mum a hug. "Hi, Mum, how are you keeping?" he asked.

"I'm fine, James, how are you doing with catching this serial killer? I hope you're resting properly and not losing too much sleep," she said, concerned. "Listen, I hope you children have a lovely catch-up time tonight," she said, giving James and Laurie a big hug each.

James didn't have much to say to his dad, so he decided to say nothing more, all that needed to be said had been said years ago and he had never really forgiven his dad for cheating on his mum.

James and Laurie drove to the restaurant where they were greeted by Prakesh, the owner. "Mr James and Miss Laurie, such a long time since we see you in here, please, I have a lovely table just for you both," he said.

"Thank you, Prakesh," said James, and they ordered drinks and their dinner.

"I want you to tell me truthfully, how are things progressing with this serial killer?" asked Laurie. "Are you any nearer to catching him? Is it getting any safer for me to go out on my own?" she said.

"I really don't want to talk shop please, Laurie," said James. "And I can't discuss the case with you, anyway," he said.

While they talked about life and other things in general, they both agreed that his sister needed to get out of the east end of London and find herself a more lucrative job, perhaps a new magazine would employ her to do their marketing. Laurie asked James if he knew any contacts that would be helpful to her but he didn't so she decided she would find new employment on her own.

Laurie got up to go to the bathroom, passing a guy sitting on his own. As she passed him, Laurie was aware that he had been staring at her most of the evening and would make sure that James was made aware of this fact when she got back to the table.

When she entered the bathroom, she heard a man's voice — *how odd,* she thought but decided to stay inside the toilet cubicle as she was a bit wary that this was not a normal situation. She heard the man go to each of the cubicles searching for someone she thought and when he realised that whoever he was after was not there, he went out. *Oh my God,* thought Laurie. *Perhaps he was drunk and thought it was the gent's toilet.*

When she got back to the table, she noticed that the man had already left. *Perhaps he had paid his bill,* she thought. Laurie told James about what had happened, and he also thought it rather odd and suspicious too. He asked Laurie if he could remember what the man looked like, but she said she didn't really take that much notice of him, except to say that he was quite good looking and had sandy coloured hair with a good physique!

*Typical Laurie*, thought James. He asked Laurie to come to the police station in the morning and see if she could put together a photo-fit of the man. It may be the break they had been waiting for.

James and Laurie went back to his office and he organised someone to take her to the photo-fit room.

WPC Dent approached James' desk and said, "Sir, your sister seems to be doing very well. She seems very observant and has come up with a small 'snake' tattoo on the man's right wrist, which she saw when she turned to look at him at the door of the ladies' room. It may be a long shot, considering the distance from the table he was sitting at and the ladies' room, so it may turn out to be a grey area."

"Okay, okay, let's just see what we get from Laurie," said the DCI.

WPC Dent walked back to her desk and felt that perhaps James was not very happy at the moment.

James's phone rang. "Hello, DCI, how can I help you?" said James.

"Tell your lady friend to ignore me otherwise she'll be next," said the voice.

"Who is this?" said James, indicating to WPC Dent to get a trace on this call. "What are you talking about and why should I take any notice of what you say?"

"Because if you don't, she'll be next." The caller hung up.

"Damn," said James. "Did you manage to trace the call, WPC Dent?"

"Sorry, sir, but he wasn't on the line long enough," she said.

James slammed down the phone but was seriously worried about his sister's and WPC Dent's welfare now. This killer was clearly not happy that someone had actually caught him out — he was getting sloppy.

When his sister finished the photo-fit she was taken to James' desk. "Hi, how did you get on?" said James.

"Okay," said Laurie. "I think the photo-fit is more like the guy that I saw in the restaurant," she said.

"Great — hopefully, we can put out an APB for him and get him behind bars ASAP," said James.

He gave Laurie a big hug and held her extra tight. Laurie was wondering what was wrong as James had not shown any brotherly affection towards her for some time.

James had a look at the picture of the guy — medium brown hair — no distinguishing marks on his face, fairly round face — fairly average looking white male — *not easy to find,* he thought — *great!*

James drove his sister back home to his parents and stayed for a cup of tea and a chat with his mum before he left for the office again. James had warned Laurie to be extra vigilant and careful and not to go out alone at all. Laurie loved how her brother cared for her — it was very touching.

Barry, the forensic technician, said they had not really got anything on this young red head girl. He said she was mid-twenties about five feet two inches tall and had well-manicured nails and obviously had money, as her clothing was all designer. They had found a small scrap of material about two inches, which may have been ripped off a jacket she may have had or the killers, nobody knew as there was no jacket or matching item of clothing on her. He said there was nothing under her fingernails and no scratch marks on her body, so again, this was going nowhere.

James was getting more frustrated by the minute and decided to speak to his captain, Max Stoller, to see if he would consider a plan he was putting together. As he walked towards the captain's office, he bumped into WPC Kelly Dent, who he thought he would love to bump into more often but hey ho, work comes first.

"Oh, so sorry, sir," Kelly spluttered, obviously feeling an idiot as she too, had feelings for the DC but knew he couldn't possibly be interested in her, a mere WPC.

"Sorry, Kelly, would you be around for a little while as I may need to include you in something I am going to put forward to the captain, if all goes well, we may need your assistance," said James.

"I will be at my desk filling out forms, as usual," Kelly said.

DCI James Bolton knocked on the captain's door and entered.

# Chapter Thirteen

Captain Stoller was a tall man with very strong facial features including a handlebar moustache, which was the brunt of many jokes in the office. "What can I do for you, James? How's it going with the serial killer? Any further news? Give me some hope that we are nearer catching this monster," said the captain.

"We've had a slight breakthrough with regards to a piece of material we have found at the scene but which doesn't match any part of the victim's clothing so it could be off a jacket she may have been wearing or the killer's clothing. Anyway, I have an idea that I would like to run by you, get your thoughts as to whether I can organise this or not," said James.

"Okay — let's have it then," said the captain.

"Well, I would like to put one of our WPC's out on the streets — I know we have thought about it before, but now this killer is getting out of hand and we really need to do something more constructive. I have someone in mind but need your approval. I thought she could be wired up and go on a party spree with my sister, Laurie, to catch this guy," said James.

"Sounds a good plan, but you know what the media will make of it should anything go wrong, they will be after our blood and more," said the captain.

"I know, I know, but it will all depend on whether this particular WPC is willing to help out, it will be quite dangerous territory and I don't know if she is prepared for this," said James.

"Okay, well, bring her in and we'll discuss it all and see what she says," the captain said.

James rang downstairs to WPC Dent's extension and asked her to come to the captain's office ASAP.

When she walked into the office, James felt his heart skip a beat, which really surprised him as he didn't think his feelings were at that stage yet!

## Chapter Fourteen

WPC Dent had been in the police force for nearly three years now and was getting to a point where she thought she would like a career upgrade. She had always worked hard and kept her nose to the grindstone and the opportunity she was being offered and explained to her now, although dangerous, gave her the impetus to move forward within the police force. She had always wanted to do homicide or CSU, so this was a great opportunity for her.

"Now, WPC Dent, we have to ask if all the facts we have given, you understand fully, especially the danger element involved. You will need to be vigilant and aware at all times and report anything you feel is suspicious at all," said James.

"Oh yes, I fully understand, DCI, and I am grateful to be given this opportunity to show I can rise to the challenge," she said, calmly, although feeling terrified inside!

"Right, I will have to meet with you and my sister, who will be accompanying you on the evening we arrange this, so how about seven thirty p.m. at Hogan's bar around the corner?" said James.

"That sounds great, sir," said Kelly keeping her response strictly business. She was wishing it would be more though!

James, Laurie and Kelly met at seven thirty p.m. prompt at Hogan's bar to discuss the forthcoming 'sting' they were preparing.

## Chapter Fifteen

Sarah called Robert back and said why not meet at his flat on Friday and could she stay for the weekend. Robert said that would be great and said he would cook a meal for them.

Robert had just arrived in the lift at his floor, at his flat that he rented from Steven, when he passed Krista, Steven's cleaner, coming towards the lift. He gave her a cheeky wink. "How are you doing?" said Robert.

"Great, how are you?" she said. "I thought you were avoiding me, are you busy tonight?" she asked.

"Not really," said Robert. "Why?"

"Well," she said, pressing him against the door of the lift. "Now that you mention it, my boyfriend is out of town and I'm feeling a bit lonely, why don't we be lonely together?" she said, feeling his hardness against her. "We could meet at the bar around the corner at about eight p.m., what do you think?" she said.

"Sounds like a plan to me — see you there and don't be late," said Robert. As Robert started to walk towards his flat he noticed Sarah walking towards him — he remembered that Steven had told him that he had someone who uses the flat at weekends but it was only five thirty p.m. on Thursday so he had better sort out something ready for the weekend with Sarah (she didn't know that Robert was staying in Steven's flat during the week) Robert said, "Hi, what you doing here, are you waiting for me?"

Sarah said, "Can we talk, please, before tomorrow night, I really need to get something off my chest."

"Fine by me," thought Robert, and such a nice chest as well.

Sarah knew that Steven was renting this flat out to Robert, but Robert didn't know Sarah was having an affair with Steven as well. Too many secrets — *about time someone took responsibility,* Sarah thought.

Sarah and Robert went into the flat. He said he did have another engagement tonight but that could wait — *after all,* he thought. *Sarah was much more interesting than Krista.*

Robert offered her a drink. "It's a bit early in the evening but what the hell — double G&T please," said Sarah.

"Go for it," said Robert. "Now, what is so important it can't wait till the weekend?" he asked.

"Sorry to bother you about work but I really didn't want to wait until the weekend to discuss this, but Steven says he is putting you forward for the promotion in the USA. Did you know he had offered me a partnership as well? Don't suppose he told you that, did he? Sorry if I sound bitter but I am furious, that's all," she said.

"Listen, I have no problem with what Steven is doing — he obviously has a bigger plan for both of us. Anyway, it's nice to see you out of hours — so to speak. What are you doing tonight anyway?" Robert said.

"Nothing much," said Sarah, knowing she was meeting Steven in three hours but, what the hell, he could wait, Robert was far more interesting anyway. "What did you have in mind?"

"Well, perhaps we could have dinner out or order in some food," he said. Suddenly his phone rang, it was Steven telling him to use the flat for the weekend as something had come up.

Then Sarah's mobile rang as well; it was Steven cancelling tonight and telling her that something had come up at home so he wouldn't be able to meet her at the flat. *What an idiot!* thought Sarah — *His loss, my gain — bring it on, Robert,* she thought.

"It looks like my friend who owns the flat is not going to be here this weekend, so how about it. How about we go for dinner at The Ivy tonight followed by drinks back here and who knows what may happen?" he said, giving her a wink.

"Hell, you're straight to the point," said Sarah. "I'll go home and change into something more suitable for The Ivy," she said.

"Why don't you freshen up here, there are women's clothes in the wardrobe, my flat mate has a girlfriend who leaves clothing here — if you get my drift," said Robert.

"Oh, okay — hopefully she's the same or similar size," said Sarah. *What a schmuck!* thought Sarah. *He will be so easy to play, it's about time Steven was taught a lesson on how not to use work colleagues against each other* — she would enjoy this farce she thought.

Robert started to run a bath for Sarah and poured her a red wine, as she didn't want another G&T, she insisted on a bath before they went out. Sarah's plan was never to go out to eat in the first place, she would make sure Robert wanted her more and more and food would be the last thing on the menu.

Sarah came out of the bedroom with a very thin dressing gown on (her own, like all the clothes in the wardrobe). She walked towards Robert and made sure that the cord around the gown was loose, in order to reveal her long legs and just a little bit of flesh to get him well and truly hooked. She pressed against Robert as she went through the doorway and could feel how hard he was — *Wow, something at last to look forward to!* she thought.

Robert took that as an invitation to come on to Sarah and grabbed her arm and turned her around making the dressing gown fall to the floor revealing her incredibly beautiful body. Sarah grabbed his shirt and took it off him, then ran her hands down the inside of his pants. Robert had read all the signs right, she wanted him as much as he wanted her, and he was going to enjoy fucking her senseless.

He grabbed her in his arms and carried her to the bedroom where he stripped off the rest of his clothes and laid her on the bed, spreading her legs and arms. He reached down into the side drawer and took out some handcuffs.

"Whoa," said Sarah. "I'm not into kinky sex," she said.

"Okay, turn over," said Robert. "And I'll show you what I can offer you."

He fucked her, thrusting so hard that she thought she was going to split open at one point, but, wow, what a lover. *This guy has it all... looks and a big cock... what else could he offer,* she thought.

They fucked all night long, with Robert only breaking for a small time to kiss her in places she never knew existed. Steven would never be the same for her, this guy was a fabulous lover and all thoughts of using him against Steven were slowly rescinding with Sarah.

Robert fondled Sarah's breasts throughout their love making and it was such a turn-on for her. He seemed to know exactly where to excite her on her body. Robert commented on her ample breasts and asked if they were her own. "Damn right they are, and don't you forget it," said Sarah.

After what seemed an endless night of passion, Robert asked Sarah if she would like to do it all again this weekend. Sarah asked if he intended going into work this morning, and he said he would probably need to but would call Steven and see how things stood.

# Chapter Sixteen

Robert got up to go to the bathroom when the doorbell rang — who could be here at this time of the night — when he opened the door it was Krista standing and demanding why he stood her up — she had waited in the bar all night.

"Well, I have someone here who turned up at the last moment — I was just getting ready," he lied. "Perhaps you would like to make a threesome? I'm sure we can work something out between us — after all, we're all adults," he said to Krista.

Krista stopped in the doorway, she wasn't averse to trying out something different; she always did like variety. She calmed down and walked into the bedroom where Sarah was lying on the bed. *Wow*, Krista thought she was gorgeous. *I could have fun here.*

After a weekend of heavy lovemaking, Sarah decided to go home to her flat. She said goodbye to Robert and told him to watch his back. Krista came up to her and gave her a big kiss on her lips, whilst fondling her breasts at the same time. "Hey, little lady, why do you have to go? Stay and let's have some more fun," she said.

"Sorry but enough is enough. As much as I've enjoyed myself this weekend, I need to go home now. But thanks for a great time."

"Okay, come on, Robbie, we still have time to spare." Krista winked at Robert and signalled she was going into the kitchen to make a coffee.

Krista told Robert that it was fun with Sarah and Robert said, "Yeh but she's gone and you're here, come on let's drink up and go have some good fun in bed."

"Why bother with the bedroom?" she said whilst removing her top and panties. "Come on, let's do it here on the floor, wherever," she said.

Robert kissed her all over again and she did the same to him, taking him by mouth and then stopping just before he reached orgasm inside her. Robbie assumed that Krista was on the pill and never took precautions. This was her plan all along: to get pregnant. Krista had been in love with Robert for several months now, but she didn't want to do anything to spoil it, so pretended that it was just a quick fling. Robert, on the other hand, thought Krista was just a quick fuck and nothing else — Sarah was something special and he would need to be careful with her feelings.

## Chapter Seventeen

Steven felt that the conversation between him and Sarah had ended abruptly and he felt unhappy at that; he went home to his wife instead of having the weekend with Sarah at the flat. He wished he hadn't cancelled it now but had to go back and try to make amends with his wife.

As he opened the door to his house, he thought how quiet the house sounded, no children running around, and no wife shouting out for him; something wasn't quite right, he thought.

"Sasha, where are you, honey? I'm home, where are you, love?" he shouted.

Steven was now getting concerned. She should be here with the children. He searched each room but couldn't find any trace of his wife or children. He decided to wait at least until eight p.m. before he would phone the police to report her missing.

He went into the kitchen and noticed there was nothing cooking or any preparation for their dinner. Perhaps they all went out and they were going to have a takeaway instead.

Steven went into his bedroom and after a quick shower, he went downstairs and decided to cook himself something, he forgot how hungry he was, and he also forgot his insatiable appetite for sex. His wife, Sasha, wasn't interested in making love any more. He thought *I can't stay in on my own tonight*, so he went back upstairs and changed into something more suitable. He grabbed his keys and went out again.

# Chapter Eighteen

He decided to ring Sarah but realised that she wouldn't be around — probably made other plans as he had cancelled this weekend — so he headed for Soho. *Plenty more fish in the sea,* he thought. *Anyway, it's only one night.*

He saw a bar and headed for it. When he was seated at the bar, he rang Sasha's mobile but got no answer — how odd. He decided to put it all out of his mind and focused on the young pole dancer with the enormous tits. He preferred older women as they had greater sexual experience and sometimes a bigger sexual appetite than his and could always make him happy in more ways than one. Steven started to reminisce about how he first met Sasha and decided he was going to marry the boss's daughter, no matter what. Well, he had achieved that goal okay, but Sasha proved not to be the best in bed — too boring and not adventurous enough for him.

His eyes settled on a beautiful brunette at the other end of the bar who looked up at him as well. She had a gorgeous smile and was very beautiful, perhaps his luck was in tonight.

The brunette, known to her friends as Kelly, flipped her hair to one side and spoke into a small microphone attached to her dress, so small it was not visible to the human eye.

"Think I may have found someone who fits our photo-fit," said Kelly. "I need to get closer — oh, wait, he's coming over, will keep in touch," she said.

"Well, hello there, lovely lady, can I buy you a drink?" said Steven.

"Why, sure, I'll have a G&T please — only a single," said Kelly.

"I'll have a G&T and a double scotch please, bartender," said Steven.

Steven took Kelly's arm and moved her over to a free booth where he sat very close to her. He was now feeling extremely horny and just wanted to screw this young lady senseless. "What's your name?" said Steven.

"Kelly," she said. "What's yours?"

"Steven, married man with three kids, soon to be divorced, sooner rather than later but hell, you don't need to know all that, what about you?" said Steven.

"Oh, nothing much, I work for a Private Investigator, boring unless we get a wife or husband asking us to follow their spouses for evidence against them — not really interesting," said Kelly.

"Wow, that's very interesting," said Steven. "I may need your services soon," he said, slurring his speech now. He had already downed two more doubles in the short time he was with Kelly.

"It's a bit dangerous for an attractive woman like you — what does your partner think of you doing a job like this?" he asked.

"Oh, I don't have anyone," said Kelly.

*Oh, the evening was getting better and better,* thought Steven.

Steven thought Kelly was a very intelligent woman, probably in her late thirties. He wondered why she was doing this type of job — he also wondered why she was alone in the bar — ah well, the night was still young, and he hadn't heard back from his wife and Kelly was a very interesting lady.

After several drinks, he asked Kelly if she wanted to go for a drive or even a late-night movie, she declined the movie but asked if Steven would drive her home. She excused herself and made her way to the ladies' room, where in the cubicle, she spoke into the microphone inside her dress.

"He's asked me to go for a drive tonight and late-night movie, I've declined the movie and asked him to take me home," she said.

"Okay, but be careful," said DCI James Bolton, who was not happy about using one of his WPCs as bait for this killer (if he was the killer). "Keep the receiver open at all times so we can hear everything — good luck," said James. He liked Kelly — she was a gorgeous blonde, the brunette wig didn't suit her at all but he was aware that the killer liked blonde women and he didn't want Kelly out there as a blonde — to tell the truth, he had fallen in love with Kelly when she was transferred to the Yard last year but he had never let her know his feelings towards her because these killings had become so important to him and he knew that he should really do this sooner rather than later.

James made sure he was very close to Kelly's wire before they both left the bar. He was in his car across the road from the bar waiting to see Kelly and the guy leaving.

However, what James didn't know was that Steven was parked behind the bar premises and as he had too much to drink, he left his car and ordered a taxi for them both.

# Chapter Nineteen

Kelly was concerned about getting into a taxi with a complete stranger, who may be the serial killer, but she was confident that she was being monitored and besides, James wouldn't let anything happen to her — would he?

When she was seated beside Steven in the taxi, she gave the driver James's address. Steven's hands were all over her body — jeez, this guy couldn't wait to get her into bed, so she pushed his hands away.

"Heh!, come on, I just want a little feel, you know no strings attached. You have such a gorgeous body and I would love you to hold it against me — as the song goes," said Steven.

"All I want is a ride home — perhaps you can come up for coffee — let's see how the evening goes," said Kelly, not feeling terribly confident though.

"Okay — just come over here," he said and pulled her towards him, kissing her very passionately on the mouth and then going downwards towards her breast. Kelly was starting to get turned on by his actions and responded by letting him feel his way up her thighs and start to use his fingers to play with her. Kelly had to remind herself that this was business and this guy was a suspect so although she realised, she had to pretend to be responsive to his playing, she realised she wasn't very good at pretending and this was all going too fast for her.

Hell, he was not the guy she wanted to make love to, that was for James only (if he ever bothered to look at her like that). Anyway, she was being turned on and decided to go with it, so she didn't arouse any suspicion from Steven. Before she knew it, he was inside her and Steven brought her to an orgasm — *hell where did that come from*, she thought.

The taxi driver was keeping his eyes strictly straight ahead but was wishing he could have some of what this guy was getting.

When they arrived at James' flat, Kelly got out and Steven paid the driver.

"Wow, nice place," he said. "Been here long?"

"A few years," said Kelly, hoping that James had removed all evidence of his stuff from the flat.

When Kelly got to the door of the flat, she pushed the door open and Steven followed her in.

"Look, I hope you don't mind but I share this flat with a friend — who is a guy — no strings attached just friends, so you may find clothing of his around. Just thought you should know," said Kelly, covering all angles.

"I don't mind sharing you, young lady, what's he like, is he around later, you know, I don't mind a threesome, whatever floats your boat," he said.

"I don't do threesomes or kinky sex, okay?" said Kelly, feeling a little concerned as to where he was going with this.

"Okay," said Steven. "Perhaps a coffee and a little more of what we had in the taxi would be great, unless you have something better to offer."

Kelly agreed and went to make the coffee, trying to keep herself calm remembering this was just a job. Whilst she was deep in her thoughts in the kitchen, she never heard Steven come up behind her and with a quick grasp of her hand he swung her around and cleared the kitchen table pushing Kelly onto the table. With his free hand, he started to remove her panties, pushed himself on top of her and entered her, thrusting and pushing very hard, certainly not as gentle as he was in the taxi. Kelly went to scream as all this had taken her completely by surprise. His actions were so swift and precise, she knew he had done this before and now she was really scared that it was getting out of hand and she was not in control any more — *was she ever in control*! she thought.

Kelly reached an orgasm that she had never wanted to experience. They reached orgasm together, but Kelly made no attempt to push him off her, she was surprised to find that she was enjoying this experience immensely.

After Steven got off her, he went into the bathroom. When he came out, Kelly had made the coffee and was sitting, dressed, on the sofa.

"I'm so sorry," he said. "I don't know what came over me, you are so sexually arousing, and I was feeling so horny around you, seemed like the natural thing to do."

"It's not a problem, just a bit unexpected, especially after the drive over in the taxi — you were like two different people," said Kelly. "You just caught me off guard, please stay and talk."

Steven found himself telling this complete stranger everything about his life, wife, kids and work, something he had never opened up to anyone about, but this lady was different and genuinely interested in him — another first in his life. Women usually just wanted the sex or money — even both but were never interested in him — she was different and he liked that.

Kelly listened to Steven and came to the conclusion that he was not the serial killer, a great stud in the bedroom but not a killer. She told Steven she needed to go to the bathroom. Once inside, she spoke to James through her wire and told him that he was not their guy. "He's been opening up to me — we've got the wrong person," she said. "Look, you can have your flat back, I'll be going home now."

"No, stay there, I'll be over once he's left," said James.

"Okay," said Kelly.

## Chapter Twenty

When she went back into the lounge, Steven had gone, leaving a note apologising but he had to get home. Kelly phoned James on his mobile and told him Steven had left so James drove back to his flat. He was keen to be with Kelly and tell her how he felt, something he should have done when he first knew how he felt about her.

Kelly opened the door to him, and James's response made her blush.

"Wow — you look great. Have I told you how beautiful you are, WPC Kelly?" he said.

"Not recently," she said. James offered Kelly a drink. She had a double scotch with him.

James walked up to her to remove the wire she had on her dress, after doing that he slipped the straps of her dress off her shoulders and then her breasts, revealing her two best assets. James couldn't help thinking, *why have I waited so long to get to this point in time with her.* She was everything he had wanted in a woman and he had wasted precious time concentrating on this serial killer instead of what was right in front of his eyes — quite literally!

James pulled her dress down her body and Kelly stepped out of it wanting this moment never to end. She was hoping that James would be everything she had anticipated and expected of him.

He gently laid her on the bed, and she started to remove his clothing as well. He was so gentle in comparison to Steven, but she would never let James know all the details — would she?

James climbed on top of Kelly and entered her, first very gently and then with more emotion and thrust until finally they came together with an enormous explosion — *Oh my God!* thought Kelly. *James certainly knows how to satisfy a woman without being brutal. I knew I loved him for a reason.* It was everything she had dreamed of.

James couldn't believe what he had just experienced — what a fool he was, for waiting so long. He knew he was in love with her and needed to let her know now. They made love for most of the evening and finally, Kelly said she would like a drink, which James brought to her in bed.

"Oh my God, James, I didn't know you wanted me like that," she said. "That was so beautiful, and you are so good in bed, you, sly old dog."

"I hope I wasn't too pushy, but I have wanted to make love to you for months now, but never thought you were interested," he said.

"How wrong you have been, James," she said. "I have wanted you just as much but I'm only a WPC, why would you even look at me?" she said.

"We can worry about that at a later date," he said. "Right now, all I want to do is make love to you over and over again, you, gorgeous girl — come here," he said, chasing her round the bed.

James told Kelly how much he loved her, and she wondered if in the clear light of the morning, he would still feel the same way.

# Chapter Twenty-One

Sasha decided to take the children to her mother's, she needed to get away from Steven. There were decisions she had to make, and she didn't want any discussions with Steven about them. She admitted to herself that her marriage was over and enough was enough. She had known about Steven's adultery for years but had decided not to do anything until the time was right for her. She had found out that Steven had been having an affair with his latest paralegal, Sarah, and as she had grown quite fond of Sarah during their meetings within the office, this was the last straw.

She drove to her mothers in Hertfordshire. As usual, her mother gave her the third degree, what was she thinking; she was throwing away everything; he would leave her penniless — *oh yes, say it like it is, Mum, always thinking in terms of money, never what I really want.*

Eventually, her mother calmed down after Sasha had told her what had been happening for several years and how she had kept it all inside, never telling anyone about Steven's sexual fantasies and how she was expected to fulfil them. Her mother looked genuinely shocked and then got very angry that Sasha had not confided in her when these events happened so many years ago. They talked over some of the issues that would arise as Steven was a very influential solicitor and would not give up easily, at least, that was what they both decided.

Her mother reminded her that she had fifty per cent control of the company as it was originally her father's business and Steven had saved it from going into bankruptcy but only if he could have the other fifty per cent control as well, which, at the time, seemed okay as they were getting married. Sasha wanted Steven out of her life completely, without any strings or clauses attached to their divorce. She decided that she would see her mother's solicitor and discuss what needed to be done.

Later that evening, she decided to get in contact with some of her old friends that she had let slip by during her years of marriage and who Steven was not comfortable with. She called her best school friend, Becka, and after much chatting to catch up with Sasha, Becka said she was having a party that weekend and she was welcome to come along and get back into the 'human race' so to speak.

Sasha asked her mum if she would be okay looking after the children at such short notice, but her mum insisted she go and enjoy herself and not to worry about them.

For the first time in so many years, Sasha felt her life was just beginning to start again. She could put Steven and his ego behind her and look forward. She took enough clothing for a sleepover as Becka had suggested it would be just like old times at college, wouldn't it. Sasha had to agree that the excitement was building inside her and she felt like a butterfly that had been given an extra life.

When she arrived at the party, she was blown away with the plush surroundings, Becka had obviously done well for herself; it would be interesting to find out where the money came from, especially as Becka's parents were never that wealthy. "Stop it," she said to herself. "You're beginning to sound like Steven, oh my God, that man's thoughts are even in my head, well, I can soon stop that," she thought.

Sasha had decided to wear a very sexy, long red silk dress which draped her beautiful body showing every sensuous curve, especially her breasts, which were always a magnet to men — sometimes it could be a pain but not tonight, she thought — *if you got it, girl, then flaunt it!*

Becka came running over to her. "Look at you, girl, you look like you just stepped off a Vogue photoshoot! You look gorgeous-you, sexy lady. Come and meet some of my friends, I'm sure you'll be centre of attention, as usual — just like college!" Sasha knew that Becka was not being sarcastic with these remarks, she had always been such a good friend, always honest and Sasha wondered why she had ever grown apart from their friendship.

"There's the bar, help yourself and I'll find the rest of the gang and bring them over," said Becka.

For some unknown reason, Sasha started to feel less confident than when she arrived. *Perhaps this wasn't such a good idea after all*, she thought. *Who was she kidding, married — soon to be divorced with three kids, who on earth would be interested and was she really looking for anything that permanent again? — Oh God,* she thought. *I need to get out of here —* too late, here was Becka.

"Ladies, this is my best friend from college, Sasha, looking as lovely as ever. Please make her feel welcome and take care of her," she said, with a wink of her eye. "You know what I mean, girls!"

They manoeuvred Sasha to the bar, where there were some great looking guys, then ordered her double vodkas and coke. Sasha was used to wine but thought, *Oh well, I'm here, I might as well enjoy myself* and downed the double vodkas. In less than an hour, she had drunk more than she could remember but was having such a ball, she didn't care.

Some of the girls asked her if she wanted to go on to another fortieth birthday party of a friend of theirs and Sasha said, "Why not — is Becka coming as well?" But she never heard the response.

She remembered getting into a limousine and someone carrying her overnight bag, but the rest was a grey fog for her. When they arrived at their destination, all of the girls got out and all were extremely drunk by this time as well, especially after the drinks in the limo — *that was so cool,* thought Sasha.

When she walked into the room, it was filled with men and women all of whom were obviously having a great time. Sasha started to dance to the music with some guy she doesn't even recall, and he was getting very horny. She thought, *Ooh, I like this feeling.* Then something happened, she doesn't remember what, but she was given a drink and taken upstairs to one of the bedrooms. She didn't resist, in fact, she found she couldn't resist and perhaps she didn't want to resist. Her friend, Becka, was there but she doesn't remember seeing her in the limo. *Hell, who cares?* she thought.

Becka came over and sat down next to Sasha, who by this time was starting to sober up a bit, although still very much intoxicated. "Hey girl" she said. "What's going on? Thought you were my best friend but then you go and leave my party, taking all my friends with you, naughty, Sasha, naughty, naughty, naughty!"

"You know, we never did get to take our friendship to the next step, did we, always swotting the law and nose in your book, well, tell you what, let's make up for those lost years, Sasha, shall we? What do you say if we kiss and make up?"

Before Sasha could say or do anything all the girls formed a circle around her whilst Becka started to take off her dress and kiss Sasha on the lips passionately, almost as if she had been waiting several years for this very moment.

To her amazement, Sasha was not as repulsed as she thought she would be but started to sober up very quickly. She pushed Becka to the ground and shouted at her, "What the hell do you think you're doing? I came to you as a friend, to talk and catch up on old times and to talk about my loveless marriage, and you are trying to molest me — what are you thinking?"

"Well, what harm am I doing? After all, your husband obviously prefers other women otherwise you wouldn't be here and I don't see any guy on this bed, so assumed you were up for anything, so, how about it? Try something different and see how you feel in the morning — what'ya say?"

Sasha didn't know whether to feel disgusted or not, but she was genuinely confused. Becka had brought out something she hadn't felt in so many years — a sense of longing that needed to be fulfilled.

"Okay, get me another drink and I'll tell you how I'm feeling," she said. "But no tricks, what I want to feel has got be genuine and not coated with alcohol, now, come over here and let's start again," she said.

Becka told the other girls to leave the room and, at first, the two friends just talked about everything the years that had passed and what life had to offer them both. Sasha was surprised to find that Becka had two failed marriages behind her and was not planning on a third. She couldn't have children which was probably a factor in both divorces, but she didn't care anymore, she wanted to live the rest of her life with people she cared about and who cared about her. She had loads of alimony from her two failed marriages so didn't have to worry about that.

Sasha and Becka talked long into the night and into the next morning before they both fell asleep.

When she woke the next morning, Becka was already up and had cooked her breakfast. She came around to the back of Sasha and kissed her tenderly on the back of her neck. It was clear to Sasha that Becka had never experienced true love from one person and was struggling to keep the situation on an even keel without giving out the wrong signals to Becka.

After having a shower, Sasha told Becka that she was going to divorce Steven and Becka warned her to be careful because as a man he would use every trick in the book to get some dirt on her so he wouldn't have to pay anything and perhaps even take away custody of her children trying to prove her to be a bad influence as a mother on his children.

This brought Sasha sharply awake and to her senses. No, that could never happen, she loved her kids and nothing and nobody was going to take that away from her. Sasha said she had to leave and get back home and Becka reminded her to keep in touch, especially now she knew that Becka had feelings for her. Sasha could sense Becka's eyes on her whilst she was showering and getting dressed and hoped that the goodbye would not be too emotional, she hated goodbyes anyway!

"Don't be a stranger, dear friend — you now know where I live and how I feel about you. I can't make you love me, but I will be here should you need a friend to talk to — any time, day or night. Take care and look after yourself. I'd love to meet your children — let me know if that's possible," said Becka.

"Hate goodbyes but will keep everything we talked about close to my heart. You take care and I'll keep in touch this time," said Sasha, as she waved her goodbye from her car window.

## Chapter Twenty-Two

Sasha drove home arriving around lunchtime. The children ran out with her mother to meet her. They wanted to know how the party had been, had she had fun and was Daddy coming to stay as well. Sasha by-passed that question, which her mother had noticed as well and went to the other bedroom.

She doesn't know why but she suddenly burst into tears. Who was she kidding? Was she really strong enough to go through with all the heartache this would bring to her children — yes, she was. She suddenly felt extremely empowered after remembering the discussion she had with Becka that evening and early morning. She was not going to cave in — she was a fighter, and, in the long term, her children would benefit from having two parents who loved them but didn't love each other — it had to be better than living a lie and, eventually, growing to hate each other. No, she was making the right decision. She went downstairs to confront her children and tell them all that was going to happen in the future, with her mother by her side.

That evening, she took the family to the local restaurant that she and Steven used to go to so many moons ago. When she had to go to the ladies' room, she noticed a guy at the bar who looked very familiar, but she couldn't think where she had seen him before. Then it suddenly came to her, he had been at Becka's house party. He was very good looking, but she doesn't remember talking to him, anyway, he probably wouldn't recognise her, she certainly was not dressed the same.

She got back to her table and was talking and giggling with the children when a waiter brought over a bottle of Champagne. "It's from the gentleman at the bar, madam, he said he knows you like this particular brand." She looked across and saw the man smiling at her — he did have a lovely smile.

"Thank you," she mouthed to him, and he turned back to finish his drink.

When they were getting in the car to leave, he came over to Sasha and introduced himself as Sam and wondered if she had remembered from yesterday's party. She said she saw him there but doesn't remember his name and apologised for that. He knew hers and said he would like to take her on a date or lunch wherever she wanted and whatever time suited her. She explained that she was just home for a few weeks making some life changing decisions but if he left his number, she would call him back if that was okay with him.

When she got into the car, her mother said, "Is that wise, dear? A man you hardly know."

"How am I supposed to get to know anybody if I don't let them in, Mum?" she said.

"True, but just be careful. There are so many weirdos out there and a serial killer, to boot, remember!"

"I will, Mum, besides, I have children, which will probably turn him off, anyway."

"Thanks, Mum," said the kids, in the back seat. "Nice to know we may be a turn off," they laughed. The children had known for several years that their mum and dad had problems but were hoping one of them would make a decision and it looked like it would be their mum. She had always put them first, unlike their dad. He loved them but never really showed it — just threw money at them — although that was good too but not what they really wanted. They laughed again at their mother trying to justify going on a date with a guy that they thought looked quite nice, but as Grandma said, she needs to be careful.

## Chapter Twenty-Three

Steven was feeling thoroughly depressed. He returned home after declining to stay at Kelly's for a 'dessert'. When he got home, there was a message on his voicemail from his wife telling him that she had taken the kids and gone to her mother's for a while and she would phone him on Monday morning — she had things to discuss with him. What things? — God, that woman infuriated him to the point where he always did something he regretted the next day!

He went and had a shower and went to bed dreaming of his date with Kelly. She really was so different from the rest of his usual 'girls' that he went with. She was definitely not a push-over and with such a beautiful body came a great brain as well. He fell asleep dreaming of what he would do to her when they next met.

Steven woke on Monday morning and picked up Sasha's message saying she was coming into the office early to see him and to be there. Steven showered, dressed and ran out the door. He phoned Sasha, "Hi, darling, how are you? I've missed you and the kids so much. How's your mum?"

"They are all fine," she said. "Look, Steven, we need to get together to discuss where we are heading in our marriage.

I'm not happy and neither are you, so we need to get it sorted. The children are suffering through the arguments and long-distance father they never see." Sasha was surprised at how empowered she felt, and it made her feel good. "Meet me in your office in half an hour," she said. "I'm just coming into the city and should be with you by then." She hung up.

Steven was lost for words. *Where the hell did all this come from?* he thought. She must have found out about Sarah in the office — *oh, hell, if she sues for adultery, she could take the other fifty per cent of the company, seeking me as an unfit parent and not able to run a company properly either. Right, a bit of smooth talking is required here*, he thought. *Admit to her about Sarah tell her everything and see what happens.*

When Sasha entered Steven's office, she felt stronger than she had ever done in the whole of their married life. No longer was she the downtrodden one, always agreeing with everything he said because he was the provider in the family. She held so much more power than she had ever imagined and was about to use every bit of it.

"Right," she started the talks. "I have spoken to the family solicitor and as I just want to walk away from you and everything this company offers. I am making a once-in-a-lifetime offer. You buy me out of my fifty per cent ownership of the company and the children will stay with me. You will, of course, have rights to see them on a regular basis, providing, of course, that you keep to that agreement. The first sign of you breaking those agreements, I will take everything from you. Do you agree?" she said, in such a harsh and professional manner that it quite took Steven by surprise — she truly made him quite concerned, which she relished.

"Sasha, I do not have the money to buy you out, why on earth do you think I have?" he said. He didn't like the way this was turning out, certainly not what he had expected her to say.

*She had certainly changed, and wow did she look good as well*, he thought. Steven was starting to drift off into his dream world, having sexual thoughts about Sasha before and now, he could screw her right here and now on his office table if he wanted — jeez, she was giving him a hard-on. Suddenly, Steven was brought back to reality, when she mentioned taking everything from him.

"Look, I would have to find someone to buy those shares and that takes time," he said.

"Well, you better get started and make no mistake, Steven, I won't be held dangling at the end of your strings any longer so get moving on finding a new partner or partners."

And with that, Sasha walked out of his office leaving Steven totally lost for words.

He didn't have time to admit about Sarah or other past indiscretions. Sasha didn't want to know or already knew and would use that as a beating stick later. At this minute in time, she was giving him an option — only one, mind you — but at least she didn't go for the jugular like most women would have.

Sasha left Steven's office passing Sarah's office on the way. She popped her head around the door and said, "He's all yours, Sarah, but be careful as you won't be the last one."

Leaving Sarah speechless as she wasn't sure what had happened in Steven's office. She saw his wife go into his office and had heard raised voices, mainly Sasha's but now realised she needed to talk to Steven quickly to find out what was happening.

## Chapter Twenty-Four

*It was time for more fun with the police*, thought Jeffrey. *They clearly are not taking me seriously. My phone messages to their offices, the small piece of rag left behind and telling the DCI to make sure his sister keeps her nose out of my business, they were not working. The stupid police had no idea who they were dealing with. My skills and techniques of killing my victims randomly and without any thought, are driving them nuts and I love it.*

*Don't try analysing me, you shrinks, been there, done that, got the t-shirt. Now my next victim will be a challenge.*

He loved watching DVD's showing murder and mayhem. After all, nobody cared about him, he had not had the treasured upbringing that some men had in their lifetime. No, he had been cast aside by society and left to rot in an asylum where nobody ever got out — except him, of course, and they all thought he was dead, any way!

*Jeffrey, I got that name off one of the coats of the wardens at the asylum before I gave him a very peaceful end to his life. He had always had such fun with me, sodomising me and getting me to do such awful things to some of the female inmates, which I eventually got to like. That's where I got my thirst for female mutilation. They are such easy pickings and such suckers for flattery. There was only ever one female in my life that I loved and that was my mother but even she didn't want me after Dad died.*

Jeffrey sat down on his sofa in his flea-ridden apartment in the east end of London trying to recall times when he was a happy young man living with his parents in Whitechapel until that awful day that changed his life.

He grew up overnight and has never looked back. He hated young women, like the ones his father used to screw at every given opportunity and decided then, that they would pay the price of his mother's demise and so would his father, as well. Though he didn't know that at the time.

## Chapter Twenty-Five

Jeffrey grew up in foster care when his mother died and then his father (nobody ever questioned their deaths — even when they were only six months apart). The police thought he had taken his own life grieving over the death of his wife. Little did they know — the fools.

When he reached eighteen, Jeffrey decided that he had enough of foster parents and it was time for him to move on. The last foster parents were glad to see the back of him. The father was uneasy about this young man's unhealthy behaviour towards his wife, always running errands and doing things for her, probably a substitute Mum since his mum died when he was only a teenager. Anyway, Jeffrey was glad to be out of there as well, good riddance, he thought.

He found a job working as an apprentice in a local garage, the only thing his father ever did was let him help in his garage and Jeffrey was a quick learner and found himself actually enjoying his new found skills working for a friend of his dads who was looking for cheap help. Jeffrey worked there serving his apprenticeship and qualifying as a mechanic in the trade. With the money he saved, he decided to put himself through law school and fulfil his long-term plan to become a very well respected and well-known solicitor in London.

It was hard work putting himself through law school and university and he studied hard, played hard and saved all his money in order to reach his end goal. Whilst he was studying and working hard, he joined a local gym and found working out very therapeutic but also made him realise that women couldn't keep their eyes off him. At first, he was a little embarrassed but later as his body became more developed, he knew he had a weapon he could use to his advantage. Women were so stupid, they actually thought that "all body meant no brain" — how wrong they were, and he made sure they knew it when they first went out on a date with him. Sometimes he got a bit rough but most of them seemed to like it so he would push more and more. He realised at a very early age that females got him aroused very quickly so it was over fairly soon and with some women that was too soon. He needed to learn how to go the mile and not come too soon — it was an art and he was learning it well.

By the time he was twenty-seven, he was a qualified solicitor working in a very prestigious law firm in Holborn, London. Helping put criminals in prison. Ultimately, this was what he wanted but secretly he had another desire which he knew he seriously needed to get help with.

Jeffrey brought himself back to the present, a long way from his beautiful apartment in Chelsea to this one in Soho. What had gone wrong? Was he to blame? They all said he was. The public, the police — he had lost everything because some woman lied about him. Well, she certainly paid the price and would never lie about anything ever again, he had made sure of that.

It was an office Christmas party at the firm in Holborn, several years ago, which had a deciding factor on his life change. One of the paralegals, Sonya, was coming on to Jeffrey and had been doing so for several months. She was further up the ladder within the company and had been taunting Jeffrey with innuendos all evening and in the end, Jeffrey had seen the red-flag and went for it like a bull. They kissed and cuddled in the lift all the way to the top penthouse rooms (only God went there and certainly not uninvited) where she told him it would be okay as they were all at the party.

Sonya very quickly had taken off nearly all her clothing and was starting on Jeffrey. She was like a woman possessed on heat, rampant were words that came to mind at that time. They both fell on the sofa in the main suite and she noticed the hard-on that Jeffrey had and as quick as lightening, he was inside her before he even knew what was happening. He couldn't stop fucking her, he thought she would drop from exhaustion, but no, this woman was insatiable, her sexual prowess was like nothing he had ever experienced before. Being a few years older than him, she had the upper hand and showed him ways to make a woman happy that he only dreamt about. This continued for nearly an hour or so until they both fell back on the floor exhausted, or so he thought.

Sonya got up, got dressed and started to walk out of the penthouse, leaving Jeffrey with just his dignity to cope with. He asked her where she was going and she didn't reply at first but then said, "Thanks for the ride, it was fabulous, we must do it again some time. Merry Christmas." And she walked out of the door.

Jeffrey was astonished; is that how it should have ended? He was still in a daze. He had never had sex with an older woman who so obviously was just using him. This made him angry and he ran after her. She had just got to the lift and was about to go back down when he held the door open and stood beside her.

"Well, that was some experience," he said. "Was that something you do to all the younger guys at Christmas or was I something special?"

"Well, you are sort of gorgeous, but I have wanted to have you since you started here with no strings attached so don't make too much of it," she said.

Jeffrey realised that this bitch had basically used him for her own fun, and he was not a happy bunny. He grabbed her arm, perhaps more roughly than he wanted but just the same it was not fair, and he was going to make sure she remembered him once and for all. He ripped her dress from her body and ran his arms up her thigh reaching the goal he was after. This bitch was going to pay for her callousness towards him as if he was nothing — *bloody whore,* he thought. *Well, now she would know what it was like to have sex with a man who didn't really want her, just her body. He dropped his pants and threw her on the floor of the elevator which was still going down. Jeffrey decided to do an emergency stop on it.* He wasn't thinking properly just had revenge in his heart for this bitch. He hit her in the face when she started to scream and when she passed out, he raped her over and over again not really thinking about his actions or the consequences it would entail. She was still out cold when he realised that the alarm would have been raised when the emergency button was hit in the lift. He redressed her body and straightened out her hair the best he could. He needed to think of some excuse when the lift doors opened, hopefully, she wouldn't be awake so he could bluff his way out by saying they were both a bit drunk and had a little 'party' of their own in the lift. This seemed the best way out of trouble, he thought.

When the lift doors were finally opened, Sonya was still out cold, and he draped his arm over her to look as if they were propping up each other. The onlookers were sympathetic, little knowing what had taken place.

Jeffrey put Sonya in his car and drove to his flat in Chelsea. He left her in the car, removing her mobile phone and locking the doors so she couldn't get out. He shut the garage door so her screams couldn't be heard — after all, his car was in basement of the block of flats so nobody would have heard her, anyway.

Jeffrey felt as if he was flying — he never felt so good about anything and it worried and surprised him at the same time; feelings that were totally alien to him. He decided he needed a plan to get rid of Sonya before she started blabbing to anyone, after all, she had started the party so what she got was justified he kept telling himself.

He slept reasonably well that night and when he got dressed for work, he went down to the garage to find Sonya awake and crying on the back seat.

"What have you done, you bastard, you raped me, you fucking raped me! I will make sure you never work in this company again. Do you hear me? They will all know what you did!" She shouted at him.

"Well, good morning to you too, Sonya. First of all, the onlookers present at the time of your so-called rape would disagree with you. They all thought we had too much to drink and had a party of our own in the lift, so it would be pretty difficult to prove any of that. Even DNA wouldn't prove anything because we had consensual sex previously in the penthouse, or have you forgotten that so quickly? Clearly, your reputation has preceded you again. Most of the onlookers just made a 'tutting' sound as if to say, 'Oh, it's only her doing her usual Christmas banging.' No, I think the time for you to stop using young men to satisfy your lusty appetite for sex has now got to stop or I will stop you permanently, do you understand?" he said, with a tone that seriously worried Sonya. She decided to play her pouting sad look face hoping that Jeffrey would fall for her sorry please and let her go but he wasn't having that at all. There was something very dangerous lurking in his eyes and it scared her to death.

Jeffrey told Sonya he was going to drop her off at her home and she should get showered and dressed ready for the office and he would pick her up and walk into work together as a couple to stop any rumours happening that morning. Sonya agreed the plan was good, after all, she wasn't about to lose her job over this jerk, but she would make damn sure he lost his, she was just as devious as he was only, he would find that out when it was too late. After all, she hadn't been sleeping with the chairman for nothing, this job had its perks, which Jeffrey would find out, all too soon.

On arrival at the office, they both went to their separate offices, Jeffrey making sure Sonya didn't speak to anyone until then. He was concerned she would try something but decided that she had probably learnt her lesson now. Oh, if he only knew what she was actually planning.

Sonya immediately phoned up to the chairman's office asking his secretary to make an appointment to see him urgently today. She arrived at his office after lunch at two p.m. and locked the door behind her. She sat down and told him what had happened in the penthouse yesterday evening (leaving out the bit where she had basically raped Jeffrey) telling him only about what followed after that in the lift. She didn't hold anything back saying that he had forced her to the ground and after knocking her unconscious he had raped her several times brutally and she said every time she started to come round he would hit her again, hence the bruising on her face. She said that she was sure that Jeffrey would go quietly but she wanted to make sure he never ever worked with any law firm again. She told the chairman that she was sure he would understand especially as they had such a close relationship and she wouldn't want anyone to find out about that either. The chairman was relieved that she was okay and understood what she was getting at. He didn't want the firm brought into disrepute by such an incident going to the media so he said he would speak to Jeffrey later that week giving him time to make a good case for his dismissal without dragging his or the firm's name through the mud. After all, he had as much to lose as anyone.

On Wednesday, Jeffrey was summoned to the chairman's office wondering what was going on. He was about to sit down when the chairman said, "Jeffrey, I'm sorry to have to do this but it has come to my attention that your workload has not been very satisfactory and that there have been some complaints from fellow paralegals about your standard of work. Whilst we consider you a valuable member of this company, I'm afraid we have to let you go. There is a very reasonable remuneration package included in this letter which I am sure will be of use to you. I am so sorry about this but please accept this as notice of your termination of employment with this firm as from today. Please can you clear out your desk and leave the premises as soon as possible."

Jeffrey was so flabbergasted; he didn't know what to say. However, as he turned and walked out of the office he noticed Sonya at the end of the corridor with a smirk on her face and it suddenly dawned on him what an idiot he had been thinking she wouldn't take it further, she obviously had the boss in her knickers as well. *Okay,* he thought. *Your time was coming, you bitch, and it would come when you least expect it. I too know how to play games!*

Jeffrey went home and threw his office possessions onto the floor of his flat. He didn't have a job and would soon not be able to afford this flat but, hey ho, he had been through worse times and come out the other end.

After several months of trying to get into another law company, Jeffrey decided that he had not only lost his job, but Sonya had made sure he had been blacklisted as well with other law firms. So, this is how she liked to play.

*Well, bring it on, lady — you've met your match, just watch out and watch your back!* he thought.

# Chapter Twenty-Six

Looking back on his life, Jeffrey realised long ago that women were attracted to him. When he worked in his father's garage, the women used to bring in their cars and always ask for him to service their vehicles. He soon found out what sort of service they were requiring, and he certainly gave them what they asked for, although, in fairness, he found both sexes appealing. Some of the guys he hung out with at the gym knew how to have a good time and they were less hassle than the women, not so demanding of his attention, just happy to take things one step at a time. *Yeh*, he thought. *Those were the good old days.*

Jeffrey collected his thoughts about Sonya and decided that he needed to teach her a lesson she would never forget — she would know how it feels for someone to lose everything. He had an overwhelming desire to take her life but thought better of it — he needed to make a strategic plan so she would never be missed anyway. *Besides*, he thought. *It's a big world out there and so many women just begging for attention!*

Jeffrey decided that it was time for a change in his profile regarding his victims. He would now target brunettes — he already had one in mind and she was a real looker, pity he missed her at the restaurant. Well, he would show her, trying to get the police to trap him. He had a shower and went out to the restaurant again to try and find her.

# Chapter Twenty-Seven

Sarah went into Steven's office following his wife's departure from his office. She decided it was time for Steven to promote her to Senior Partner or give her an equal share of the partnership. *After all, hadn't she serviced him well?* she thought.

Steven was sitting looking out of his office window. *What a cow!* he thought. *How dare she think she could just make a decision about his life and his children?* After the initial shock of what Sasha had proposed, he decided that all is fair in love and war and he had better make the right decision here now.

Sarah slammed his office door and came over to Steven and sat on his lap. "What are you playing at, Steven? I thought you were going to offer me the promotion, but I've found out from Robert that you've offered him the promotion as well, what's going on? Don't you want me at your side as an equal partner, in every possible way?" she said.

Steven was not in the mood to be brow beaten into any further decisions of his life and work status. He pushed Sarah off his lap and told her to meet him at the flat later that night around seven thirty and he would let her know what he intended to do about everything concerning her, her career and the company. He was in no mood to talk business now, he had things to sort out. Sarah was not happy but agreed to come around to the apartment tonight. She would make sure things went her way this time.

When she went back to her office, Robert popped his head round the door and asked if she was doing anything tonight, she said she was busy and what did he have in mind, knowing how much she was really falling for Robert, Steven was just a means to an end in her career, nothing more but Robert was different. He turned her on in ways she could only dream about. *To hell with it, I'll put Steven off and see him tomorrow, tonight was Robert's night.*

"Well, I was wondering if you would like to go back to my place for dinner, I just thought that after our lovely weekend, we could do the same again, what do you think?" said Robert.

*Hell*, thought Sarah. *I only have the use of Steven's flat on Fridays and Saturdays when I'm with him, Robert has no idea I am the other woman in Steven's life.* She needed to tread carefully she thought, she liked Robert and wouldn't want to mess things up.

"How about we go out to dinner and go back to your place after?" she said. Sarah thought this would give her time to blow off Steven and leave him without his usual sex at the weekend with her, which was getting to be a bit of a bore now.

"Great, I'll book us a table at Luigi's Italian in town for seven thirty, okay?" said Robert, and he walked out of her office with a big grin on his face.

Sarah phoned Steven and told him that she wouldn't be around this evening as something had come up, but she definitely wanted to see him later next week to sort things out.

Steven didn't argue or protest, he had other fish to fry and Sarah was getting to be a bit clingy, he really needed to do something about her, but what? he thought.

Sarah went home to her flat that evening and spent a long time making sure she made herself so enticing that Robert would have a hard time resisting her advances. She wore the red dress he so obviously liked, which showed all her assets to the world. Hell, she felt good and was feeling so sexy she couldn't wait to get him into bed with her again!

## Chapter Twenty-Eight

DCI James Bolton was dreaming about WPC Kelly Dent, who he realised had now got a large part of his heart forever. He was in love with her without any doubt and was not happy about using her as bait any more. Kelly had also said that the guy she 'picked up' at the bar was not the person, he didn't make any attempt to grope or even have sex with her. James started to day dream about Kelly, after all-their one night of passion didn't mean she was ready for a full on commitment, she may not be interested in long-term, especially as he's a DCI and would be out all hours of the night — probably not something she could deal with, anyway, he would ask her outright what her long-term vision was about them, if there was a 'them'. James was suddenly brought back to reality with the phone ringing.

"DCI, how can I help you?" he said.

"I told you to forget any photo-fit of me, but you didn't listen, so on your head be it, DCI," and the caller rang off.

"Wait, what do you mean?" said James, but the caller had hung up.

He asked the sergeant if WPC Dent was at her desk or on the beat.

"She's in the canteen, guv, do you need to speak to her?" he said.

"Can you ask her to come to my office?" said James.

When Kelly arrived, James felt a rush of pure adrenalin through his veins, wow, she did that to him every time he saw her. James had called another meeting of the special victims unit (SVU) and asked if there was anyone else they could use as bait this time, making the excuse that Kelly was probably now known to the killer. However, Kelly spoke up quite loudly saying that she was happy to be bait once more and would prefer to be given the opportunity again.

James was not expecting that, thinking she would be happy to step down and not take risks again but how wrong he was. He admired Kelly for her bravery but thought it best to try someone else and shot her down in seconds with his decision.

Kelly asked to leave the room and went back to her desk. She was furious with James; how dare he ignore her request as if she didn't matter. Was this the same guy who had sex with her a couple of days ago or was she just another notch on his DCI belt. She felt hurt, humiliated and angry all at the same time. What a fool she was to assume he would even consider her for a second chance. *Wake up and smell the coffee, Kelly*, she thought. He's a high-ranking officer, why would he be genuinely interested in her any way she thought and sat down and got on with her reports to fill out.

James left the briefing room after the meeting finished and came to find Kelly at her desk.

"I'm so sorry for not choosing you again, but I thought you would want to give someone else a chance, in case the killer recognises you and this would put you in the forefront of potential danger again. I wasn't happy to take that chance, also the killer was obviously at the restaurant that night as he just phoned my office and told me to forget the photo-fit, if we didn't, we would regret it, that's why I made my decision," said James.

"You weren't happy, how dare you use me, make love to me as if it was nothing and then give this job to someone else, maybe another WPC you have the hots for," she said quietly to him but wishing she could shout at the top of her voice about what she was feeling right now.

James stood back, really shocked at this outburst, he thought she would understand that he didn't want her to be put in harm's way, especially the way he felt about her. He said if she wanted it that bad then she could be the bait again, but this changed nothing between them. He had told Kelly that first night that he had felt something for her the first time they met at the station but never pursued anything because of his position but was blown away when Kelly told him how she felt about him, so this outburst really hurt James and he wasn't sure how to deal with it but if Kelly wanted to be bait, he wouldn't stand in her way. He told Kelly to go to the SVU and they would brief her on all the details about the next sting. He then turned around without any further words and walked back to his office. *Women*, he thought. *You try to protect them but no they want to be heroes, well, so be it, if his feelings of concern for her weren't enough for her to stand down, then who was he to argue.* James was feeling very hurt at this moment in time.

Kelly didn't know how she was feeling, elated that he had backed down or fearful of the outcome between her and James. She knew she loved him but would this be the same if they took it to the next level, she wasn't sure if she was ready for that yet, but then again, he was a great lover and oh so much more, she thought. *Oh well*, she thought. *I suppose I better play it by ear and see where this goes.*

## Chapter Twenty-Nine

Kelly met the other WPC, Suzy, who she was going to the restaurant with — they would both be potential 'bait' but Kelly decided to wear her brunette wig again and advised Suzy to just be her usual blonde colour. "OMG, I've never done undercover work before," said Suzy, who was clearly excited to be doing this. "Hope I don't let anyone down. You must know how I'm feeling, especially as you did this last time as well," she said.

"Nah, you'll be okay, Suzy, just remember to act normally, don't bring attention to yourself, it would make the situation a bit obvious, especially to the killer," Kelly said.

The girls met in the locker room at six p.m. after they had finished their beats. Both had decided to wear something 'sexy and inviting' as Kelly had put it. They needed to attract the killer but be physically able to get out of a bad situation, so nothing too close fitting or restrictive.

When Kelly and Suzy arrived at the restaurant that Kelly had been to the previous time, Kelly ordered them a couple of drinks at the bar before they sat at their table. They had both been wired with special microphones placed in the inside of their handbag handles so nothing too conspicuous.

Kelly noticed Jeffrey at the end of the bar (of course, she didn't know his name was Jeffrey, he was kind of cute though, she thought.)

"Hey, can I buy you two lovely ladies a drink?" said Jeffrey.

"No thank you, we've just got these," said Kelly and turned her back on him.

This made Jeffrey even more determined to get to know these ladies. *Probably out for a good time tonight, well, they'll get that all right*, he thought and walked back to his end of the bar, keeping a watchful eye on them and liking what he saw.

The waiter came over to Kelly and told them that their table was ready, so the girls left the bar. As they walked to their table, Jeffrey watched them closely. *Wow*, he thought he really did want to get these two in bed with him — looks like tonight could be a good night after all. Just as he was settling down to his thoughts and his drink, who should walk in but Sonya — that bitch! He had never felt such hatred for any of his victims but this one was the exception to the rule; she not only ruined his life but was strutting around as if she owned the place. He later found out that she did, in fact, have a stake in this restaurant, which he would do something about as well. How dare she ruin his evening.

When Kelly and Suzy had ordered their meal, Kelly said she would go to the toilet and see if she could contact DCI Bolton just to make sure their mikes were working properly. As she walked past Jeffrey at the bar, he winked at her and she winked back at him. *He was really cute* she thought, but business is business. She thought of James and felt guilty for having these thoughts, but he had presumed rather a lot. Anyway, she got inside a cubicle and made contact with him.

"Can you hear me, Bolton," she asked using her code name for him.

"Loud and clear, Kel," he said (his name for her). "Sergeant and I will be coming into the restaurant soon and have a table booked near the door. If we make a move on you and Suzy just play it cool, just in case the killer is watching us," he said.

"Okay," said Kelly. "I'm sorry about my outburst earlier but I was hurt by your rejection of me to do this job."

"Listen, we are being monitored," said James. "So, keep it simple," he said.

"Fair enough," said Kelly and left the toilet.

When she got back to the table, Suzy told her that Jeffrey had been 'winking' at her and giving her the 'eye' so to speak.

"Great, that's all we need, a pervert, he may stop the killer from making a move," said Kelly.

The girls stretched out their meals for as long as possible, hoping that someone would make a move, but nothing happened. Just as they were about the pay the bill, the waiter brought over a bottle of champagne and said it was from the man at the bar, the one who tried to buy them drinks.

They raised their glasses to Jeffrey and said, "Thank you." They looked across at James and the sergeant so they were aware of who had brought them the drinks.

Kelly and Suzy finished the rather large bottle of champagne between them and before they could leave, Jeffrey came over and asked them if they would like to go on to a nightclub to finish off the evening. Both girls said why not but they would need to visit the toilet first to freshen up.

"You look great to me, but I'll wait," said Jeffrey, who was getting an incredible hard-on just thinking of these two in his bed.

Kelly and Suzy were feeling slightly tipsy at the moment and talked into their microphones saying they were going on to a nightclub, they didn't know which one but made sure they left their phones open so James could hear them.

Jeffrey met the girls outside in the lobby and they said they would get a taxi to the nightclub as neither were capable of driving.

"No need, I have my limo out the back," said Jeffrey, the one he had hired to impress.

*Wow,* thought Kelly. *He has money as well as looks.*

By this time, Suzy was well and truly out of it, she fell asleep in the limo and Kelly was aware that she was totally on her own now. She made herself comfortable on the seat and stretched out her legs — beautiful legs James had said; well, he wasn't here so what the hell. She sat back and Jeffrey was on top of her before she even knew what was happening, a bit like the previous suspect, she thought. This guy was different, he was very rough and tore her dress off her, she attempted to scream but he knocked her out. The limo wasn't moving because nobody was driving. Jeffrey had planned this to the end. He got in the driver's seat and drove out of the car park.

James and the sergeant had followed them out of the restaurant but did not see what car they got into, as it was parked round the back. By the time they had got around the back, the limo had left. James was getting worried now as Kelly and Suzy's mikes did not appear to be on.

*What the hell had gone wrong?* he thought, he couldn't lose Kelly, not now. She was everything to him and he wanted to make sure she was around to hear that. They went back to their police car and radioed in that the girls had been abducted possibly in a limo that had just left the car park– number plate not recognised as covered over — how many people had limos — *It should be easy to trace* he thought.

James and the sergeant went back to the station to try and get further information from what little had happened that evening.

In the meantime, Jeffrey had parked the limo at his premises (or his dump as he called it) and carried Kelly out first. He disregarded Suzy and just dumped her on the pavement, she was totally smashed from the drugs he had put in their drinks, but unfortunately, the brunette — Kelly — didn't drink enough to knock her out, a pity, as he now would have to make sure that Kelly couldn't identify him after he had finished with her.

He took the handbrake off the limo and let it roll into the Thames River, the police could deal with that one. He had worn gloves so there would be no fingerprints.

Jeffrey went back to his place and found Kelly starting to stir. He grabbed her arm and put her over his shoulder and carried her into the bedroom where he slowly undressed her. He got her handbag and threw it on the floor and that was when he found the microphone inside the handle as it became loose.

Jeffrey was furious, what a mug! He had been played again by yet another beautiful woman, well, she was going to find out exactly how he treated bitches like her.

When Kelly started to wake up, she couldn't focus properly as one of her eyes was badly swollen. This guy had hit her so hard he had given her a black eye.

## Chapter Thirty

Jeffrey thought he had recognised one of the men that came in earlier at the restaurant but put the thought out of his mind. *Could he be working with this girl?* he thought. *What if he was a policeman and she was being used as bait?* he thought. He quickly dismissed all those thoughts and focused on what was happening now. This girl was obviously working with the police and he would need to find out what she knew and what she had said to them earlier.

Kelly was sitting up on the bed when he walked in with a drink in his hand. He needed to find out what she knew.

"What the hell were you thinking?" said Kelly. "Didn't we both say we would come with you? Why did you have to hit me and where's my friend, Suzy? What have you done with her, you bastard?" she screamed.

Jeffrey went over to Kelly and slapped her face. "Don't you call me names, you bitch; you've tried to set me up with the police, haven't you?" he said, raising his voice. "Want to know what happened to your friend, I'll tell you. Once I had my wicked way with her, I dumped her on the side of the pavement, she'll not remember much and probably won't talk about it for years to come. She was a great fuck and so very cooperative," he sniggered to Kelly. "You know what I mean!"

Kelly was screaming inside for her friend and colleague but tried to hold it all together now that she was awake. She started to make a mental note of her surroundings, taking in the lack of furniture, and obviously he was not as rich as she first thought when she got in the limo with him. He looked as if he was struggling to make ends meet and she wondered if he was the killer or if this was another dead end. He may be a nutcase she thought but it doesn't make him a killer. He didn't seem to fit the profile of what the police were looking for. After all, the killer preferred blondes and Kelly was a sort of blonde but not a real blonde and besides, she was still wearing her wig, he hadn't noticed it was fake so obviously not very bright either she thought.

Jeffrey offered Kelly a drink, no thanks she said remembering her last drink he had given her and Suzy. She wanted to make sure she was fully alert now.

"Have a drink now," he said. "You will be dehydrated otherwise and no good to me at all. I was hoping for a threesome, but your friend declined my kind offer so it's just you and me, babe," he sneered at Kelly.

Kelly said she would have some water and nothing in it. Jeffrey left the bedroom and whilst he was gone Kelly looked for her bag to see if she could find any way of contacting James and letting him know what was going on. Whilst she was looking for her bag Jeffrey came in with the microphone in his hand. "Looking for this," he said. "You really need to tell your friends not to listen in to your conversations, it's very naughty and makes me very angry to think someone could be listening to everything I say to you and do to you."

Kelly now realised the potential danger she was in and started to get off the bed before she realised that there was no way he was going to let her go. She started to scream at the top of her voice but realised that the room had been soundproofed, even though it didn't look as if he could afford to even have that done, she thought. Then she realised that she may never see James again and this saddened her to think that she left without saying a kind word to him. She started to cry and Jeffrey came over to her and put his arm around her saying not to worry it will all be okay, and with that he hit her on the head with a baton he had under the bed and knocked her out. Kelly was out cold now and there was nobody there to help her, not even James.

Jeffrey lifted Kelly up and placed her sitting up on the bed. He wasn't sure how he was going to deal with this one as he was worried that the copper may have got a good look at him when he was at the bar in the restaurant, although he was pretty careful to keep his back to the tables only turning to raise a glass to the two girls and when he met them outside the restaurant. He wasn't too concerned, he had to re-think his plan for the evening and what he intended doing to this lady so she wouldn't recognise him again, ever!

He went outside to the shed, or rabbit hutch as he called it, to get his tools. He would need to make sure no evidence was left on her to trace back to him. Shame really, he thought, he quite liked her and was definitely going to have sex with her one last time, no way was she making a fool of him again.

He picked up a plastic sheet and his 'tools' and walked back inside the flat. *That was a joke,* thought Jeffrey. *This was no flat just some pokey bed-sit that he had made look reasonable so he could bring girls back here.*

Kelly was still out cold, so he laid her down on the bed and got a condom out of his bathroom cabinet and put it on. He hated these things, but it prevented DNA from being traced.

He started to undress Kelly and was amazed at her beautiful body, especially her breasts which were perfect and so real, not plastic like those other snooty bitches he used to know a lifetime ago. He gently started to play with her nipples and caressing her between the thighs, which got him to reach an early ejaculation — shit! He wasn't expecting to come so quickly. He went and got another condom and started the process all over again and this time he entered inside her and thrusting and pushing harder and harder he finally came inside her. Kelly had started to arouse now and when she found him on top of her she went to scream but Jeffrey put his hand over her mouth and silenced her, telling her not to scream otherwise he would rape her again and again.

He got off the bed and got some rope, which he tied Kelly's hands to the bedpost and her legs he separated and did the same. He went and got a flannel and stuffed it into her mouth so her screams could not be heard. Kelly was petrified now and thought this was the end of her life as she knew it, she tried to struggle but to no avail she was bound and gagged without anyone coming to her aid.

Jeffrey came back from the bathroom where he had disposed of his condoms and applied a fresh one again. He was an animal tonight he thought and was loving every moment of it. He straddled himself over Kelly dangling himself near her mouth and teasing her with his hard-on. He was surprised as to how quickly he had become hard again. This woman certainly did things for him that he had never experienced, such a shame she won't be doing it to anyone else he thought.

He moved downwards and started to kiss Kelly between her thighs, arousing her to the point where she tried to scream but could not be heard. Kelly couldn't help but get aroused as this was a part of the lovemaking that she had experienced with James. It suddenly dawned on her that it would never happen again, and she started to sob quietly to herself.

"Hey, little lady, don't cry," said Jeffrey. "I won't hurt you, just want to fuck you senseless, you have such a great body and I want to hold it against me," he sang to her. He had an erection that was starting to hurt him now and thrust himself inside Kelly and kept on thrusting until she finally passed out again. "Shit, what you do that for?" said Jeffrey. After what seemed to be hours, Jeffrey finally fell asleep next to Kelly, who was still bound and gagged. Kelly came to and found Jeffrey fast asleep, thinking this could be her chance to escape. *Escape where,* she thought. *How the hell was she going to get out of here!* And she started to sob again.

When Jeffrey awoke, he decided that he was finished with Kelly and needed someone different now. His sexual lust was his biggest downfall; he just couldn't stop himself. He was probably more like his father than he wanted to admit. He decided to give her a drink of water laced with Phenobarbitone, which he had used in the past for his other victims. He was starting to get the adrenalin rush that he always got when he knew what he was going to do to his victims but this one would be different; she could recognise him and he had only one choice to make. He would then leave her where she could be found, after all, he had actually liked this one but still had to do what he had to do, he thought.

## Chapter Thirty-One

DCI James Bolton was feeling extremely worried now as to the disappearance of both of the WPC's. Kelly being his main concern, of course, in hospital but also that of WPC Suzy. Both girls had appeared to have gone missing, even their mobile phones could not be traced to them via their GPS. They must have been dumped or destroyed. He was so distraught that his CO told him to go home and they would contact him if there was any further information or news.

James went home and kept going over the last conversation he had with Kelly which was tense, and words said by him had been misunderstood. All he wanted was to say he was sorry for being such an idiot and he was only thinking of her, but all this would be too late if anything happened to her.

He tried sleeping that night, but he kept seeing Kelly hurt or worse and it was a nightmare for him.

The phone rang the next morning and when he finally got to it, it was Suzy. She said that she couldn't remember what had happened to her and didn't know where Kelly was either. She was crying down the phone and said she was at the police station looking at mug-shots but could not find the man they were with that evening. She said she had been drugged and possibly Kelly too but couldn't be precise about that either. James told her not to worry and that he was heading off to the police station now.

While he was driving, a police message intercepted in to his phone advising that a woman had been discovered on Blackheath Common and was on the point of death when the ambulance arrived. James floored the accelerator of his car and got to the hospital ASAP. He asked if there was any further news of the woman, her name etc., the young nurse on reception said her name was Kelly and that's all she could say. She had been beaten up pretty bad but the worse news of all was that her eyes had been removed. The procedure had not been done professionally and there was further trauma to the young woman's body as well. James asked the nurse if he could see the young lady called Kelly. He said he was her DCI and she was under his protection. James almost fainted when he saw Kelly lying in the hospital bed. She had been sexually assaulted and god knows what he had put her through but at least she was alive, if only barely. He stopped himself from throwing up in the bin next to him and sat down by Kelly's bedside.

## Chapter Thirty-Two

Jeffrey was on a roll, he decided to go to Soho after having dumped Kelly's body. He needed a 'fix' so to speak and there were plenty of opportunities in Soho — *Bring it on*, he thought. He tried to remember when he became as depraved as he was and decided it was his wife's fault, she was always so strait-laced and never wanted to be adventurous, yes, it was definitely her fault, she was the reason for his depravity of women in general.

He found a bar called Diamonds and went downstairs where he gazed upon several young women who were pole dancing. Jeffrey thought the night was still young and there was plenty of opportunity here and took a seat nearest the front of the stage. He salivated over a young girl, she looked about twenty he thought, just ripe for plucking he thought and set his mind to how he would get her into his bed tonight. He could feel his passion coming to a climax and he hadn't even got her into bed yet — *Jeez*, he thought. *I need to control this before I get caught!*
Jeffrey was still enjoying himself at the Diamonds night club and the young girl he had his hard-on for, was called Melanie. *Lovely young filly,* he thought. *And great body, well, she*

*wouldn't be here if she hadn't got a good body,* he thought. *Pity his wife had always been such a strait-laced prude, her loss not his,* he thought.

He asked Melanie if she would be interested in spending some quality time with him — *Yeh,* he thought. *Quality time!* — after she finished worked and offered her a drink. She said she was up for that but would have to advise her boss as she shared a flat that was owned by the boss and she could be funny about where her girls went after work. Jeffrey said to ask the boss if she wanted to join them, he was happy to do a threesome! Melanie said she would ask but didn't think she would take up the offer.

About eleven thirty p.m. after Melanie finished work, she met Jeffrey in the car park in his limo, which he could tell easily impressed the bimbo, he thought. What a night he would have with this young filly, oh yes, he was so aroused he found it hard to keep it together for just a little while longer. The night was long, he thought.

Jeffrey drove Melanie to his apartment, where he was sure she would be no trouble at all. Jeffrey and Melanie drank copious amounts of drink in the limo, although Melanie's drinks had all been laced with his usual drugs to make sure he got no resistance. When they arrived at Jeffrey's apartment, Melanie was so drugged she could hardly stand, and she had a sense of being scared as she had never been drunk like this before. She asked Jeffrey if he felt okay and he said he never felt better.

Jeffrey almost carried Melanie to the front door of his apartment, which he had cleaned up after his experience with Kelly; it didn't look as if anything had happened at all.

He put his arm under Melanie's arms and carried her to the bedroom, where he promptly tied her hands and feet to the bed posts, after which he started to undress her. At this point, Melanie was not even stirring now so he undressed her very quickly before looking at her naked body one more time before he decided what he would do to her. He felt totally and utterly depraved and wanted her so much, he needed to fulfil himself.

Jeffrey decided not to use a condom, he wanted to thoroughly enjoy himself and they always felt so constrictive — bloody things, but then he realised she had probably slept with other men and may not have used any protection and he certainly didn't want to catch anything either! So he decided to wear a condom on this occasion.

He threw some cold water over Melanie to try and awake her, he wanted her to see and hear what was going to happen to her and this made him even more aroused.

## Chapter Thirty-Three

Melanie stirred a little but not enough, he needed to see the fear in her eyes and also if he aroused her at all, which does happen sometimes he had found. So, he threw some ice-cold water on her and this made her open her eyes even more. She tried to get free and Jeffrey was pleased to see the fear in her eyes as she struggled with her legs as well, such beautiful long erotic legs which he could see were begging him to climb all over her, oh well a man has to do...

He let Melanie scream for the first few minutes and then decided to gag her, he couldn't stand the noise and needed to concentrate on what he wanted to do to her. Melanie had become totally conscious now and her fear and terror were adrenalin to him. She tried to take on board what was happening to her and realised she had no way of getting out of this situation so decided to go along with this animal, hoping he would at least let her go after he had raped her, which is what he was doing now as she would definitely not be consenting to anything he was doing to her, it was too horrific.

Jeffrey decided to play with Melanie's beautiful hair stroking it tenderly with his hands and working his way down to her breasts, which he caressed and decided he would have an orgasm in between them, to which he came several times before he climbed off her to start somewhere else on her body. Melanie was disgusted and scared so much as she was not able to stop anything he was doing to her now. She felt dehydrated and sick at the thought of what he was going to do next.

Jeffrey got down from the bed and decided to go and get another drink, which seemed to boost his erection even more; whoever said booze dampened their erections hadn't met Jeffrey, he was something special, he thought!

When he came back into the bedroom, he brought a glass of water for Melanie, but she said could she have an alcoholic drink instead, a strong vodka and tonic. Jeffrey said okay and thinking he would let her have one hand free to drink it, she was disappointed to see he had put a straw in it. This guy had thought of everything. She wondered what the time was and asked him to which he responded it's still early he said, only one a.m. She asked if he would let her go, once he had been satisfied with her performance to which Jeffrey replied, "We'll see."

After continually raping Melanie and making her take his penis in her mouth several times, he finally felt fatigued and needed to rest. Melanie was tempted to bite his dick on several occasions but thought better of it as she wasn't sure what he would do to her after that, so complied and took him several times in her mouth, after which she felt very sick.

# Chapter Thirty-Four

James was feeling completely helpless as he now had no possibility of Kelly ever recognising her assailant. The killer had poured acid into her beautiful eyes and left her in such a bad way that she was in ICU at St. Thomas's Hospital in Westminster fighting for her life. Her life as a WPC was well and truly over and all in the line of duty — bloody joke that was! He was getting more and more angry that this killer was out there and wouldn't stop until they had caught him or killed him — the latter being exactly what James was craving. His love for Kelly would be put to the test now assuming she still wanted him around at all.

The sergeant opened the door of Kelly's room and asked if he wanted to take a break, to which James replied no. "Has there been any further breaks as to where we found her and any nearby house-to-house searches for anything?" James said.

"Sorry, sir, no further developments — he seems to have disappeared into thin air," said the sergeant.

"I hope I don't get my hands on him first, no telling what I will do to him," said James.

"I'll pretend I didn't hear that, sir."

"I don't care who hears it," said James. "The bastard deserves everything I will give him and more."

## Chapter Thirty-Five

Jeffrey woke at six a.m. feeling fed up and bored with his latest conquest, she had served her purpose and he would need to make sure she could never recognise him again. Whilst he had been sleeping, Melanie had also had a chance for her body to be rested although she knew he would start all over again. This time she was worried when he came into the bedroom, Jeffrey had decided she would have to be drugged again before he could do anything to her. He didn't want this one to suffer painfully whilst fully awake, like Kelly before her. Melanie was not trying to deceive him and didn't deserve what he was about to do to her, but it was survival of the fittest — so to speak.

Jeffrey went into his kitchen and got the tools for the job he was about to do and also an injection to put Melanie to sleep, she was a really good fuck too — such a shame!

Melanie watched him approach her with the needle and asked, "What are you going to do to me? Please don't kill me, please!"

Jeffrey said he was just going to put her to sleep, she would wake up with a bit of a headache nothing else. He failed to tell her what would happen after the drugs took effect.

After Melanie had fallen into a deep sleep (he hoped he hadn't given her too much), Jeffrey got her dressed and then poured the acid onto her eyes. He got an erection doing this and decided to fuck her once more, which had never happened before, this time without a condom, he hated those rubber things, yuk! He decided to wait until late evening before he would wrap her in a blanket and dump her on Blackheath common like Kelly.

Jeffrey didn't realise that he had made one fatal mistake this time and it would be his undoing.

## Chapter Thirty-Six

Jeffrey saw on the news the next morning, that his last victim, Kelly, had died of her injuries sustained by him. He was sad for a moment but then tried to justify his actions by her betrayal and lies. She was a good fuck and so much more, but life goes on. Jeffrey was on the hunt now for new opportunities and he didn't mean boring old work. He had managed to escape the attention of the police but was not aware that his latest victim, Melanie, had survived her brutal attack and her injuries had been treated rapidly in order to reduce the amount of damage to her eyes.

Melanie was recovering in hospital in the ICU with a policeman outside her room. The same room that Kelly had been taken to. Sadly, Kelly lost her fight to survive and James and the sergeant and the whole department involved in catching this psychopath, were now more determined than ever to find him and bring him to justice.

James was thinking I hope I find him first because he will not survive anything I do to him, he had made that promise to Kelly on her death bed.

After attending Kelly's funeral and meeting with her family, he decided that once he had caught this killer, he would jack it all in as a policeman. He had seen enough and experienced most of the bad stuff that comes with the job, but this last episode with Kelly in his life had been too much for him to bear and his decision was final. He had spoken to his superiors and they said he was too good a policeman to lose but his decision to leave when he had found the killer was something they could not stop if he was that determined.

James made his way back home to his apartment exhausted and angry. Why weren't there any more clues available for them to catch this bastard. It wasn't enough that he had practiced SM on Kelly but to pour acid on her eyes as well, this guy was an animal and deserved to be shot. James decided he needed to get hold of a gun, not one registered to the police as he didn't want anyone to get into trouble for what he was going to use it for.

Melanie was asking the policeman on duty outside the ICU room if she could meet with DCI James Bolton, as she had some important information for him and possibly a DNA test could be taken to confirm who the killer was.

The policeman rang the office of DCI Bolton and relayed the message. This was a breakthrough thought James and just what he needed to try and catch this bastard.

When he met with Melanie, she was very distraught to hear that Kelly had died but was now wanting so much to get things off her chest.

She told James that she had been raped by this man and perhaps there was some DNA still trapped in her body that could be tested, in case he's on the police records at all.

James calmed her down and said he would organise a test but would have to make sure the doctors agreed that this was okay under her present circumstances.

James felt a certain kind of rush come to him as if he was nearing his goal to catch this bastard.

## Chapter Thirty-Seven

Sarah and Robert spent the weekend together having wonderful sex, Sarah thought, with a man who showed variety and excitement in almost every aspect of lovemaking. Wow, what a difference to the normal stuff from Steven. She thought she would really have to let him down gently. Sarah didn't realise that Steven had a dark side to his nature but suspected that he wasn't everything he claimed to be. She didn't care, as long as he paid her a good salary for the job she was doing in and out of bed with him, she laughed to herself. He really was a bore and could understand why his wife wasn't interested any more. Perhaps she was having an affair as well. Anyway, she was having a great time with Robert and he was one hell of a lover, bring on some more please, Robert.

"Hey, daydreamer!" shouted Robert, bringing her back down to earth. "Do you want a drink? Or are you okay for a bit more?" laughed Robert.

"Come here, my stud, and fuck the hell of out of me, we're not finished yet," said Sarah.

Whilst they were resting in between making love, Robert asked Sarah if she had slept with Steven at all and he wanted an honest reply, no bullshit. Sarah looked him straight in the eye and lied saying only twice, once because she felt sorry for him and the other to secure her job (basically he wouldn't have given her the job and made it impossible for her to decline his generous offer). She wasn't prepared yet to reveal all her little indiscretions with Steven, after all, Robert worked for him as well.

Robert, who was feeling very relaxed and at ease with Sarah, told her some things about Steven that she made a mental note about, after all, she may be able to use this against Steven should his demand for her body become too much. *Oh yes, keep talking, Robert*, she thought.

Robert told her about when he and Steven were at Uni together and how Steven liked the boys as well as the girls but mainly how Steven had actually caused the death of one of the students. Suddenly, Sarah was all ears and wanted to know more. *This could be useful*, she thought, little knowing who Steven really was.

After a very long evening of talking and making love, they both finally fell asleep in each other's arms.

When Robert woke, he stared down at Sarah who he had to admit to himself he had fallen in love with. This woman made him feel like a man and he was going to hold onto her for as long as he could. He wondered if he should have told her everything about Steven but realised, he didn't care as Steven had used him so much in the past and it was nice for him to off-load some of his thoughts about Steven anyway.

When Sarah eventually awoke mid-morning, Robert made her breakfast in bed and lay down next to her whilst she ate it all, she said she was ravenous and laughed saying, "I can't think why!"

Robert took her in his arms and told her how he felt about her, and Sarah, without hesitation, responded in the same way. She was shocked as she realised that yes, she had fallen in love with Robert. Against everything she was hoping to achieve in her life the last thing she wanted was to feel like this. *Bugger*, she thought *But, what the hell, how bad could it get. Robert was agent, and would treat her like a lady unlike most men she had met in her lifetime. Oh well, let's go with the good feelings today*, she thought, the weekend was just beginning and she made no resistance to Robert making love to her again.

They went to the movies laughing and joking like two love-sick teenagers. Sarah had never felt so happy or Robert either and they both told each other this, which seemed to Robert as confirmation of Sarah's love for him.

The weekend went far too quickly and before they knew it, Monday morning was upon them. Robert had not brought a change of clothes for work as he didn't realise, he would be stopping all weekend, so he had to go home to his flat and get changed before meeting Sarah at the office again. It would prove a challenge to both of them when they met with Steven again for the usual Monday morning briefing — how bloody boring. Who needed these meetings anyway? All the top solicitors did their 'chat briefings' on a telephone link up with their partners but not Steven, he was too dogmatic and old fashioned in a lot of odd ways. *Ah well*, thought Sarah. *Perhaps I should wear something less appropriate for this meeting, just to tease the boys and see what happens later in the day.*

# Chapter Thirty-Eight

During the meeting, which took place at nine a.m. sharp, Steven advised everyone that he had made his decision on who should take up the senior position at their USA offices. Steven knew who he was going to offer it to anyway but kept his thoughts to himself and told the board members he would ring the lucky person tonight. "If you don't get a call, assume you didn't get the post," he said.

Steven and Robert had both noticed the outfit that Sarah was wearing, which was totally unsuitable for their working environment but hell she looked good. Her dress was electric blue with a very discreet slit up her right leg, which only stopped so close just between her thighs; both men had got an erection and were both thinking the same thoughts. Her cleavage was on full display and didn't leave much to the imagination. Sarah knew the effect this was having on most of the male members of the board and loved every moment of it. She would screw the lot of them the way she was feeling right now. How dare Steven take so long to make a decision about the position in the USA? She deserved that position and it would get her away from the UK office and Steven. She felt sad when she thought of Robert but perhaps, she could make another position for him in the USA if Steven gives her this job. He better had, was all she kept thinking.

After the meeting, Steven went back to his office and rung Robert to advise him that he was the lucky candidate, after all, he didn't want Robert in the UK telling people about his past, he would definitely lose the partnership and ownership from Sasha, his wife. She didn't need much of an excuse to find some more dirt on him and take him to court!

By five p.m., Sarah realised she was not going to get that call, so decided to confront Steven face-to-face.

She walked down to his office but was concerned when she heard Robert and Steven talking and laughing together in Steven's office. She threw the door open not waiting to be asked to come in.

"So, from the laughter, I assume Robert got the posting to USA. How very convenient, Steven, after all, perhaps you were thinking that Robert wouldn't tell anybody of your past indiscretions at uni, huh? Well, trust me, I have nothing to lose by speaking to your wife and letting her know about your sordid past, yes, that should make great reading in the national newspapers!" she shouted at Steven. "Robert, I am surprised you didn't have the decency to let me know earlier, after all, did you also let Steven know that you and I have been having sex behind his back at his apartment!" she shouted.

"Robert, is this true?" said Steven.

"Yes, it is and bloody good too," said Robert. "I love her, and she loves me, and I intend to take her to the USA and ask her to become my wife, if she'll have me," he said.

"Get married to you, where the bloody hell did that come from?" said Sarah. "We had a few nights of passion, yes, I admit I love you but not enough to get married. My career is the only true lover I have at the moment and the occasional fuck with you two guys was always a bonus, so, no, I won't be marrying you, Robert but happy to be your girl Friday/weekend," said Sarah, knowing that what she was saying was hurting Robert so much, but she was so angry that she felt totally used and abused by both of these two cretins.

Steven was now the one to be lost for words. He had no idea Sarah and Robert were together in any way and it turned him on and before she could continue with any further talk, Steven said to them both, "Well, I have an idea that may just prove beneficial to all three of us and I would like you to let me have your response now. Have either of you considered a threesome, after all, we all have feelings for each other and love sex, how about I send both of you to the USA and we have our own bon voyage party just the three of us and some other friends I know of. Let me know what you think," said Steven.

Steven's comment threw Robert off keel but not Sarah. It wouldn't be the first time he's introduced someone else to the evening's activities but this may prove more lucrative for her and Robert, it may just benefit them both as well.

"I don't need to think about it, I'm always up for a threesome especially with the two most important men in my life," she said.

"Hang on," said Robert. "I'm not so happy about it. I love you, Sarah, and want to start our married life with some true and honest thoughts. Are you saying you would do this just so you can work at the USA office? What about you and me?" he said.

"Well, darling," Sarah said, as she walked over to Robert and straddled her legs over his lap. "Perhaps we can have some pre-party fun and you can let me know how you feel about that, although from where I'm sitting, I guess I already know," she said, knowing full well he now had an erection and could hardly keep his hands off her breasts, which she pushed against his face to tease him.

Meanwhile, Steven had also got an erection and wanted so much to fuck Sarah right here and now and walked over to his office door and told his secretary the meeting was continuing in his office and not to disturb him. His secretary knew only too well not to interrupt him, she had learned the hard way in her earlier years.

Steven bolted the door and immediately went over to Sarah and undid her dress while Robert removed the front of her dress from her shoulders and took her breasts in his hands and massaged them until she could feel herself climaxing on his lap.

Steven and Robert lifted Sarah out of her dress and laid her across Steven's desk, with Robert still massaging her breasts and Steven pulling down her panties and entering her whilst she was on her back on the desk.

Sarah was totally reaching an orgasm now and could hardly contain herself from screaming with pleasure. After Steven had come inside her, Robert turned her over and entered her from behind, whilst she lay on top of Steven, who took over the massaging of her breasts. Both men had never felt so aroused before with Sarah and she was enjoying every part of it and climaxing every time.

This threesome was proving to be addictive and Sarah was actually enjoying it more than she thought she would. Steven and Robert decided it was now time for a change and told Sarah she needed to get on her knees and suck off Robert whilst Steven took Robert from behind just like he tried once at uni and was not successful. Steven had waited a long time for this and although painful for Robert at first, he enjoyed it but definitely not as much as screwing Sarah. Her moistened vagina was something he wanted to feel with his tongue and after he had come in Sarah's mouth, he wanted to taste her lips below. After Steven had finished with Robert, Robert put Sarah on her back and spread her legs so that both men could taste her sweetness down below. Sarah squealed with pleasure and wanted more of this and for it to never stop, she didn't realise she had such insatiable appetite for sex but now she found she couldn't do without it and it certainly was a tool that could get her what she wanted, especially with these two guys.

After an hour or so had passed all three lay on the office carpet exhausted and then re-dressed themselves. Steven and Robert still had erections and wondered if they could each satisfy themselves with Sarah later tonight.

When Sarah was fully clothed and standing, Steven and Robert came up to her and Steven said, "Thank you, that was the best fuck I have had in a long time, Sarah, and especially fucking you, Robert. It was a dream come true for me," he said as he winked at Robert.

Robert took Sarah's hand and asked if he could drive her home. Steven said "Don't forget, Robert, we can now have a threesome regularly at my flat, if you want. I know I certainly do and if Sarah is tired, I'm sure we could have some fun, if I bring some other pals along as well, what do you say?"

"Sounds like fun," said Robert but he was not happy about sex with Steven, it was okay but he was a woman's man and always would be, anything else under the circumstances was just a bit on the side and nothing he would take seriously. It's a pity he didn't realise what Steven's plans were though.

## Chapter Thirty-Nine

Steven had decided that he would have to let Sarah and Robert take the position in the USA. He couldn't have his wife finding out about his indiscretions, although he suspected that she had plenty of her own but he could not prove anything.

He went back to the apartment and called his wife to let her know that he would be moving his office to the USA and he would need to speak to her about this as she was a partner, so to speak.

His wife, Sasha, was furious when he said this but then thought this could work to her advantage. With Steven out of the way, she was free to finally live the life she wanted but she would make him pay dearly for the miserable creep that he was and then there was the children to sort out i.e. who would they live with etc. Yes, there certainly were a few details that needed to be sorted.

Steven read in the newspaper that Melanie had survived her ordeal and the surgeons had managed to repair some of the damage to her eyes. However, she was a long way off from being released from hospital yet and the police had new evidence that they may be able to find out who the rapist and killer was that they had been trying to catch for the last decade.

Steven was now getting very agitated and couldn't rest. He called Sarah and told her he needed to meet her urgently in his office at eight a.m. tomorrow morning.

Sarah said, "Is there going to be another threesome, Steven? You know, I quite like that idea."

"No, just get your arse in my office by eight a.m. and no later and make sure you tell Robert that as well," he said.

"Okay," said Sarah and called Robert and gave him the message too.

"I'm not happy about this sudden meeting, Sarah" he said. "What does he want to do and say now?"

"I neither know nor care less but whatever it is, he had better get us on the next plane to the USA," she said.

Robert and Sarah arrived at the office before anyone else and were there at eight a.m. sharp.

Steven was already seated in his office and told them they had to leave for the US offices by tomorrow or the post would go to someone else and this was a special favour to them as his friends. He never really told them that he wanted them out of the country so they couldn't spill the beans to any newspapers about his depraved sex life now and earlier at university, no, he was tying up loose ends.

Sarah was slightly peeved as she had to sort out the tenancy on her flat etc., as did Robert but they both agreed they would be at Heathrow airport by ten a.m. tomorrow. Steven said he would book the seats himself (his included — although they didn't know that) and leave them at the office later today for them to collect. Steven was now more afraid of the police finding him after they check their records and see he has a police record for GBH and suspected rape from his university days and Robert could probably confirm all this as well, so this was a good move he was making.

Steven called Sasha and told her he would be leaving for the states in the morning and would make arrangements for her to be well cared for and possibly sign over the partnership to her entirely, which she was quite happy with now that her life was changing too. However, he did stipulate that Sarah and Robert would be the new VP's in the USA office and she shouldn't try to intervene in this transition. Sasha said she couldn't care less who was doing what as long as the money was coming in, she was happy with that. Little did Steven know, that his soon to be ex-wife would take him to the cleaners anyway and start her life again.

## Chapter Forty
## The Finale

Melanie had undergone the DNA testing and DCI James Bolton had made sure she was safe and still under protection especially as someone had leaked to the newspapers that there had been new evidence come to light!

The tests came back as a positive match to Steven Golding — last record dated back over twenty years when he was at university and the disappearance of two girls!

Obviously, this guy had been busy! Well, now he had nowhere to run!

Steven (or Jeffrey as he called his alter ego) had booked flights for Sarah and Robert leaving Heathrow at ten fifteen a.m. for New York and himself for eight p.m. tonight. He was taking no chances on the police catching him before then. Besides, he said, "New country, new expectations and plenty of hot girls in New York, I'll bet." Steven said goodbye to his kids and his ex-wife and wished her well. Sasha thought it was very rushed, this exit from Britain but decided he was probably trying to escape making some young girl pregnant and not wanting the responsibility of it all. *No changes there then, Steven,* she thought.

Steven hired a vehicle and made his way to the airport, cleared passport control and was feeling pretty damn pleased with himself when he was sipping champagne in the departure lounge.

Meanwhile, DCI James Bolton had got a complete dossier on Steven and was driving to his home, only to be met by his wife, Sasha, who advised him that Steven was on a plane to New York on business and wouldn't be back for a while. She joked and said, "What has he done now? Made some girl pregnant or is there an angry husband chasing after him, whatever, he deserves whatever is coming to him." And with that, she laughed and shut the door.

Sarah and Robert caught their flight to New York in the morning. They arrived at the new offices fresh and ready for business the next day.

Imagine their surprise when they found Steven sitting in the CEO's chair.

"What the bloody hell are you doing here?" said Sarah.

"There is no CEO position, Robert and I are Vice Presidents of this company, you gave us your word!" she shouted at him.

"Well, there was a slight change of plans. My wife decided it was better if I controlled the New York office as the new CEO, so although you are VP's both of you, I still have control of this company, so please be courteous to my new position or we may have to come to some arrangement again, know what I mean?" he winked at both Sarah and Robert.

"Well, I didn't come all the way across the world to be demoted, I don't know about you, Robert, but I'm up for a threesome, how about you guys?" said Sarah, and with that, she shut the office door making sure they would not be disturbed and undressed herself. It didn't take Steven and Robert long to see the situation and make the very best of it.

Steven thought *I need to make sure Jeffrey lays low for a while before I go out on the town! — New York ladies, beware when I come calling!*

Steven (alias Jeffrey) would soon be making his presence known to the New York Police Department and would learn that life in New York would certainly bring him some unexpected pleasures that he didn't bargain for!!

DCI James Bolton was so angry that he had missed Steven by seconds but that didn't stop him from going to the airport, just in case his flight had been delayed. This killer was not getting away from him this time. He would take the next flight out to catch this bastard and put an end to his killing spree once and for all.